Dear Reader

Living and working in a r particular challenges for explored in this, the secc fictitious Scottish Island thriving population, many of whom you will have met before in A BRIDE FOR GLENMORE.

I love writing connected books, because they offer scope to develop characters who clearly have their own story to tell. This time it's the turn of Dr Logan MacNeil and his practice nurse, Evanna Duncan.

Since the death of his wife, Logan has been concentrating on his role as island doctor. He's also a single father, and relies on the help of his family and the islanders to juggle the demands of parenthood. Top on his list of helpers is Evanna, his colleague and long-time friend. But Evanna is struggling to keep within the boundaries of their friendship. She's in love with Logan and has been for most of her life. But she knows that the time has come for her to stop dreaming and make some difficult decisions.

Will Logan ever see her as anything other than a close friend? And, if he doesn't return her feelings, can Evanna continue to live and work on her beloved Island? Or will she be forced to leave everything she loves?

Set against the backdrop of Glenmore Island, with its dramatic coastline and wonderful beaches, this is a story of friendship and love nurtured within a small, caring community of people who want the best out of life. If Logan and Evanna can teach us anything, it's that when the opportunity for happiness presents itself it should be grabbed instantly and greedily with both hands.

I hope you enjoy their story.

Warmly

Sarah

Logan was stunned by the strength of his feelings. Nothing in his past had prepared him for what he felt for Evanna.

So much for all his resolutions about staying away from her. He'd taken one look at her in her bikini and had red-hot thoughts. So red-hot that he hadn't even been able to look at anyone else all evening, let alone dance with them.

Even now his body tightened at the memory of how she'd looked. Her hair had been damp from the water and had hung, glossy and dark, over her bare shoulders. Her eyes had been dark as sloes, her lashes thick and unbelievably long. And then there had been her mouth.

Logan groaned and closed his eyes.

Her mouth touching him—

They hadn't just shared their bodies. They'd shared *everything.*

And that sharing had somehow cleared his thoughts, and he'd realised just how much he loved Evanna. Just how much he needed her. How much he'd always needed her. Her warmth, her kindness, her endless compassion.

Her gentle hands, her soft mouth and her warm, amazing body.

He'd always thought that what they shared was all about friendship, but he realised now that it was so much more than that.

So much more than he'd imagined possible...

SINGLE FATHER, WIFE NEEDED

BY
SARAH MORGAN

All the characters in this book have no existence outside the imagination of the author, and have no relation whatsoever to anyone bearing the same name or names. They are not even distantly inspired by any individual known or unknown to the author, and all the incidents are pure invention.

All Rights Reserved including the right of reproduction in whole or in part in any form. This edition is published by arrangement with Harlequin Enterprises II B.V. The text of this publication or any part thereof may not be reproduced or transmitted in any form or by any means, electronic or mechanical, including photocopying, recording, storage in an information retrieval system, or otherwise, without the written permission of the publisher.

MILLS & BOON and MILLS & BOON with the Rose Device are registered trademarks of the publisher.

First published in Great Britain 2007
Harlequin Mills & Boon Limited,
Eton House, 18-24 Paradise Road, Richmond, Surrey TW9 1SR

© Sarah Morgan 2007

ISBN-13: 978 0 263 19796 9
ISBN-10:   0 263 19796 4

WOLVERHAMPTON LIBRARIES	
B100000000876113	
HJ	534932
	£12.25
AP	1 9 MAY 2007

Set in Times Roman 10¼ on 12¼ pt
15-0407-54390

Printed and bound in Great Britain
by Antony Rowe Ltd, Chippenham, Wiltshire

Sarah Morgan trained as a nurse, and has since worked in a variety of health-related jobs. Married to a gorgeous businessman, who still makes her knees knock, she spends most of her time trying to keep up with their two little boys, but manages to sneak off occasionally to indulge her passion for writing romance. Sarah loves outdoor life, and is an enthusiastic skier and walker. Whatever she is doing, her head is always full of new characters and she is addicted to happy endings.

Recent titles by the same author:

Medical Romance™
A BRIDE FOR GLENMORE
THE MIDWIFE'S CHRISTMAS MIRACLE
THE CHRISTMAS MARRIAGE RESCUE
THE SICILIAN DOCTOR'S PROPOSAL

Modern Romance™
BLACKMAILED BY DIAMONDS,
  BOUND BY MARRIAGE
THE SULTAN'S VIRGIN BRIDE
MILLION-DOLLAR LOVE-CHILD

CHAPTER ONE

A FRESH start.

Evanna Duncan drove her little car off the ferry, hearing the familiar clunk as the wheels left the ramp and hit the concrete of the quay. She waved at Jim, the ferryman, and then drove a little way down South Quay before pulling into a vacant parking space overlooking the harbour.

The city had been hot and sticky, the air trapped between the tall buildings with not a breath of wind to lighten the atmosphere, and she'd crawled through holiday traffic for hours to reach the ferry. She was hot, tired and desperate for the peaceful haven provided by her cottage on the cliffs. But first she had things to do. She was meeting a friend and she was already late.

Climbing out of her car, Evanna breathed a sigh of relief as she felt the wind lift her hair and cool her skin. At last.

Home.

Glenmore Island. Being a practice nurse on a remote Scottish island had its challenges, but she loved it and she could never imagine living anywhere else. She'd only been away for a month but it felt like longer.

'Good trip, Nurse Duncan?' A boy of about twelve strolled up to her, licking a towering ice cream in danger of imminent collapse. A baseball cap was pulled low over his eyes and he wore shorts, scuffed trainers and an ancient T-shirt that had been faded by endless washing. Two of his friends hovered in the background.

'Well, hello, Fraser. Are you enjoying the holidays?' Evanna slammed the car door shut. 'How's that head of yours doing?'

Fraser obligingly whipped off the hat and lifted his hair to show her. 'What do you think? Dr MacNeil says he thinks it's going to be the most *amazing* scar. Wicked.'

It was typical of Logan MacNeil to have turned a negative into a positive. Evanna ignored the way her heart jumped at the mere mention of his name. 'I'm sure he's right. Amazing.' Instinctively she reached out and took a closer look, noticing how well it was healing. *Logan had done a good job with the stitches.* 'And I hope you're staying away from the castle.'

'Sort of. But you'll never guess what's happened, it's *so* cool.' Fraser's voice was earnest as he filled her in on the local gossip. 'They've decided to open up the dungeons. Some archeologic—archolo—' He stumbled over the word and then gave up. 'Someone *really* important is coming to take a look and poke around. They think there might be stuff down there. Stuff from the Celts or the Vikings or something, you know? Like treasure. We're going to go up there and watch.' His eyes gleamed as he rammed the cap back on his head.

'That's great, Fraser.' Evanna slipped her keys into her bag. 'Just make sure you're careful. Those ruins can be dangerous and you've given all of us enough grey hairs this year. Your ice cream is dripping. You need to lick. Fast.'

Fraser grinned and caught the drip with his tongue. 'I'm careful.'

'I'm sure you are.' Evanna's tone was dry as she recalled the rescue effort that had been required to extricate him from the dungeon some weeks earlier. She flicked the brim of his hat with her finger. 'I'm meeting Nurse Walker. Have you seen her?'

'She's in the café by the window eating a *massive* triple chocolate fudge ice cream with extra chocolate flakes. She made me promise not to tell anyone because she says it's pretty hard to lecture people on eating a healthy diet when you're seen in public stuffing yourself with rubbish.' He frowned. 'Actually, she might not have actually said "stuffing yourself", but I think that's what she meant.'

'Disgraceful behaviour for a practice nurse.' Evanna's eyes sparkled with laughter. 'I'll go and tell her off, shall I?'

'Yeah. The ice cream looked good, though, and it's the only thing that really works in this heat. Bye, Nurse Duncan. See you around.'

'Bye, boys. Be careful, now.'

She was still smiling when she pushed open the door of the café and joined her friend at the large round table by the window. It had a view of the harbour and was a perfect place from which to observe the various comings and goings of Glenmore Island. 'You know, if you're going to eat that artery-clogging gloop you should at least do it behind a newspaper or at a table around the back. Eating it in the window is just asking for trouble. I've just heard all about it from Fraser.'

'You're late.' Kyla dropped the spoon and stood up to give her a quick hug. 'You saw Fraser? He's a cheeky monkey. With most of the summer holidays still ahead of us, I wouldn't be surprised if we're pulling him out of another hole soon. It's *so* good to have you back. We've missed you.'

'You've been too busy being newly married to miss me.' Evanna dropped her bag on the floor and pulled out a chair. 'I still haven't quite got over the speed with which you fell in love with our new doctor. You certainly didn't hang around.'

Kyla settled back at the table and dug her spoon into the ice cream. 'When something is right, it's right. And Ethan is perfect.' She waved the spoon. 'At least marrying him meant that he'd stay on the island permanently. Logan is pleased to have another doctor at the surgery.'

'Yes.' Evanna struggled to keep her tone casual. 'So, how is he? Logan is normally hideously busy at this time of year.'

Kyla considered the question. 'OK, I think. I don't know how he does it. It's only just over a year since his wife died but he's holding up really well. I just wish he'd talk about it more.'

Evanna thought of the conversations she'd had with him long into the night. *He'd talked about it with her.* 'I suppose everyone handles things in their own way.'

'Well, Logan always was tough and work keeps him going. That and having a thirteen-month-old daughter.' Kyla leaned back in her chair and called across the café. 'Aunt Meg, can we have another spoon here please? Evanna's tongue is hanging into my ice cream.'

'No, it isn't.' Evanna eyed the ice cream wistfully. 'I'm not like you. Fat never gives you a second glance. If I even *look* at ice cream, I put on a kilo.'

'That's rubbish and if eating ice cream gave me your fantastic curves then I'd eat it for every meal. You look great in that red top. A bit like a flamenco dancer.' She narrowed her eyes. 'Sort of sexy and sultry. All dark hair and dark eyes. But you need to wear your hair loose to complete the effect.'

'It's too hot.' Evanna ran a hand over the back of her neck. 'And the only reason I'm looking sultry is because we're in the middle of a heat wave. I'm boiling.'

'Was it hot in the city?'

'Unbelievable. I honestly don't know how people can live their lives in a place like that. It's all so—' Evanna frowned as she searched for the word '—closed in. There's no air. It's like being in a forest of buildings and everyone is busy, busy, busy. There's no room to breathe, whereas on Glenmore there's just so much space.' She shuddered at the memory and Kyla smiled.

'So you didn't enjoy yourself?'

'I enjoyed the work. It was fantastic to be back on the labour ward. You know I loved my midwifery and I don't exactly get the chance to practise much on Glenmore.'

'What are you complaining about? It's like a rabbit colony here.' Kyla waved the spoon. 'Both Sonia Davies and Marie Tanner are pregnant. And Lucy Finch's baby is only four days old, so you'll be visiting her for a while.'

'I know.' Evanna gave a soft smile. 'I actually delivered Lucy in the labour ward on the mainland. It was amazing and, of course, it's great that Sonia and Marie are pregnant. But it's hardly enough to make up an entire workload.'

'Well, Sandra King had a far-away look on her face this week and I know that she and Paul have been trying for ages, so I wouldn't be surprised if she's in the surgery soon. And we don't just want you for your midwifery skills. This island needs two practice nurses. I know midwifery is your first love, but don't even think about abandoning me!'

'I wouldn't leave you. I love it here and I love the variety.' Evanna glanced out of the window and caught sight of Janet, the practice receptionist, who was walking past, carrying two bags of shopping. She smiled and waved.

'But you love midwifery most of all. You're totally soppy about babies.' Kyla gave a wry smile. 'Go on. Has working on the labour ward made you broody?'

Evanna felt a grey cloud drift across her happiness. 'Of course not,' she lied, turning back to Kyla with a smile. 'How can I be broody when I don't even have a boyfriend? You know I believe in doing things in the right order.'

'You always were an old-fashioned girl.' Kyla watched her

for a moment and then looked up as her aunt approached. 'Aunt Meg, Evanna needs feeding.'

Meg was a plump woman with a generous smile and a mass of curling blonde hair. 'Good to have you home, Evanna.' She wiped her hands on her apron and reached for a pad. 'What can I get you? Same as Kyla?'

'Just a coffee, thanks. Americano. Decaff, no milk.'

'That's all? I've a chocolate cake that's enough to make a woman cry.'

Evanna ignored temptation. 'Just coffee.'

'And how's that going to give you energy through a long day?' Meg tutted her disapproval as she put the pad back in her pocket. 'You need flesh on your bones, lass.'

'I have flesh on my bones,' Evanna said dryly. 'I can't lecture people on losing weight if I'm overweight myself. At the moment I can still fit into my clothes and that's the way I want it to stay, especially given that it's the swimsuit season.'

'Could you stop being so perfect? You're ruining my enjoyment of this ice cream.' Kyla licked her spoon and looked regretfully at the empty dish as Meg removed it and walked back towards the kitchen. 'So—did you meet anyone gorgeous while you were away?'

Evanna hesitated. 'Sort of.'

'Really?' Kyla's eyes were suddenly interested. 'Tell me.'

'There's nothing to tell. He was a registrar in obstetrics and he was really…nice.'

'Nice? What sort of a word is *nice?* It doesn't tell me anything. Was he good-looking? Sexy? Intelligent?'

'All those things. We went out for a few drinks.'

'And?'

'There is no "and."'

'Did you sleep with him?'

'Kyla!' Evanna shot an embarrassed glance across the café

but everyone was engrossed in their own conversations. She answered the question in a low tone. 'No, I did not.'

'Shame.' Kyla was unrepentant. 'If you ask me, you could do with some unbridled passion in your life.'

'I didn't ask you, and my life is fine.' Evanna sat back and gave a smile of thanks as Meg put the coffee in front of her. 'We just had drinks. But it made me think. And I came to a decision.'

'What decision?'

Evanna blew on her coffee to cool it and waited for Meg to walk away before she spoke. 'I'm not doing this any more, Kyla.' Her voice was firm and steady. 'I'm not wasting any more of my life pining after a man who doesn't even notice me.'

Kyla's smile went out like a light bulb in a power cut. 'You're talking about my brother.'

'Of course. Who else? Who else has there ever been for me?' Evanna shook her head and gave a derisive laugh. 'Ever since we played kiss chase in the playground, it's been Logan. I've never even been able to *see* another man if he's in the same room as me. And when he's not in the same room as me, he's in my head. Even when I close my eyes I can still see him. I can see his smile, I can see that wicked gleam in his blue eyes. I can see the way he walks as if he owns the world. And it's a crazy waste of time, because he doesn't even know I exist.'

'He does know you exist.'

'I mean as a woman. When it comes to seeing his patients, making his dinner or caring for his child, he knows I exist,' Evanna said flatly. 'When it comes to anything more personal, I'm invisible.'

'He lost his wife, Evanna.'

'I know that. And I also know that it was over a year ago and, sooner or later, he's going to find someone else to share his life with. And no matter how much I dream that it might be, that someone is *never* going to be me. So I'm over him.' She said it for herself as much as Kyla. *To remind herself of all the promises she'd made to herself while she'd been away.* 'No more moping. No more pining. No more wishing for something that is never going to happen. I'm putting plan A into action. I'm moving on.'

'How can you move on? He's a GP and you're his practice nurse. We all work together.'

'Of course I have to see him at work. And of course I'll help him with Kirsty. He's had a horribly rough time and he's a single father now, so of course I'm going to help with his little girl. But I'm going to have my own life, too.' She felt the confidence rise inside her and suddenly felt strong and determined. Everything was going to be fine. After all, she hadn't seen Logan for a month and she'd survived, hadn't she? There had even been moments when she'd enjoyed herself. A few seconds when she'd managed to forget about him. And she was going to build on that. Seconds would become minutes. Minutes would become hours. 'I'm going to go out.'

Kyla raised an eyebrow. 'With?'

'I don't know.' Evanna sipped her coffee and gave a shrug. 'Anyone who asks me. Nick Hillier?'

'You fancy Nick?'

'No.' Nick was the island policeman and they'd been at school together. 'Not really. It's just that...'

'It's just that he isn't Logan. Wow. That's a really good way to begin a relationship.'

'I don't want to spend the rest of my life by myself,' Evanna said softly, resting her cup carefully back in the saucer. 'You asked me if I was broody and the answer is, yes, I'm broody. But not for a baby in isolation. I want so much more than that. I want to have a home and a family and a man who loves me, and I'm not going to find that while I'm blinded by your brother. I've been stupid about him, I can see that now. The way I feel about him has stopped me even noticing other men, but that's going to change. When I was away, I managed to talk some sense into myself. I went out with the people from the unit and had fun. It was good. And I realise now that it's up to me to build a proper life here and I'm going to do exactly that. No more waiting around and hoping. No more deluding myself. I'm really, really over him. Honestly.'

At that moment the door to the café opened and a man strolled in. He was taller than average, with lean features and a suggestion of stubble on a firm jaw that hinted at the stubborn. His hair was dark and slightly too long at the back, just touching the collar of the blue linen shirt that he wore tucked into a pair of light-coloured trousers. He had broad shoulders and blue eyes that were sharply observant, and all the females in the café turned to stare as he pushed the door shut with the flat of his hand and strolled towards the counter. 'Hi, Meg. Can I have a round of toast, please?' He spoke in a deep, sexy drawl and the coffee cup slipped out of Evanna's shaking fingers and clattered onto the table, spilling the contents.

Kyla uttered a sharp expletive and reached for a pile of napkins, dropping them on the table as she tried to staunch the flow of coffee. 'You're over him?' She kept her voice low so that no one else could hear. 'If you're over him, Evanna Duncan, why are you dropping things when he walks into a room? Plan A obviously isn't working so I hope to goodness you have a decent plan B worked out in that head of yours, because it might be time to make the shift. For goodness' sake—how much coffee was in that cup? It's like a lake here.' She mopped frantically but Evanna didn't even notice. She was too busy trying to control the frantic shaking of her limbs.

'I don't— I can't—'

'Evanna?' Kyla dropped more napkins on the soggy mess,

but her sharp whisper held a note of concern. 'You're as white as chalk—are you all right?'

No. She wasn't all right. Her pulse was thundering at a ridiculous rate and she knew that if she'd tried to stand, she would have sunk to the ground in a heap.

Oh, no, no, no! She'd thought she had her feelings well and truly under control. She'd thought—

Her thoughts froze altogether as Logan strolled over to them, a smile in his wicked blue eyes.

'So this is where both my nurses are hiding. Now that I'm here, we could have a practice meeting. It's long overdue.'

Evanna found it almost impossible not to stare. She'd always found it impossible not to stare at him. In primary school, when she'd been just five years old, she'd gazed at him from the corner of the playground—stared at the dark-haired, blue-eyed god who had come to collect Kyla from school. In secondary school she'd drunk in every detail with the dawning awareness that came with the onset of womanhood. And then he'd left the island to train as a doctor and had returned only for holidays and she'd stared at his photograph—*the one taken on the beach during the summer that he'd been a lifeguard.* His chest was bare and bronzed and he was laughing into the camera.

She still had the photo.

'Evanna.' His mouth moved into a smile and her gaze was drawn to his mouth. It was firm and sensual and, in her opinion, designed for kissing. Not that she'd know, she thought miserably as she tore her eyes away, because Dr Logan MacNeil had never kissed her and was never likely to. He'd kissed just about every girl on the island, but never her. He just didn't think of her that way. In fact, it was probably true to say that he didn't notice her at all. She was part of the island he'd grown up on, as much part of the scenery as the beaches and the mountains.

'Can I join you?' He spoke in that deep voice that always

turned her knees to liquid and made her think of sex and seduction.

'Of course. Hi, Logan.' She struggled to keep her voice casual and quickly moved her hands to her lap so that he couldn't see them shaking.

Her reaction was pathetic, she told herself. About as pathetic as hanging onto an ancient, dog-eared photograph.

Kyla scrunched up the saturated napkins and stood up to throw them in the bin, casting a long, meaningful look in Evanna's direction.

'Well, I'm certainly glad to see you home, Evanna.' Logan sat back as Meg placed the toast and coffee in front of him. 'I've missed you, desperately. Every moment that you were away seemed like an hour.'

Evanna's hands clenched in her lap and she felt an involuntary dart of pleasure at his words. *He'd missed her?* 'R-really? You missed me?'

'Yes, really. How can you doubt it?' He spread butter on his toast with those long, lean fingers that she knew were so skilled with patients. 'It's the summer. Glenmore Island is heaving with tourists and every surgery is packed. *Not* the best time for one of my precious nurses to go swanning off to the mainland for a month, even if it was part of her professional development.' He smiled the smile that had every woman on the island reeling. 'Of course I missed you. Did you think I wouldn't?'

Professional development.

He'd missed her at work. Evanna gritted her teeth and looked away from that charismatic smile. *It was always about work.* She was his practice nurse and nothing more.

She swallowed down the disappointment, reminding herself that she'd always known that. Hadn't she just spent an entire month dissecting their relationship in minute detail? Hadn't she been brutally honest with herself about the way he saw her? The answer was yes to both questions, so why did hearing him confirm her analysis hurt so much? If anything, she should take it as confirmation that she was doing the right thing. And no matter how hard it turned out to be—*and she knew it was going to be incredibly hard*—she was going to move on.

Kyla sat down again. 'Evanna had a good time on her refresher course.' Her tone was cool and pointed, and Logan glanced up from buttering his toast.

'Good.' He bit into the toast and lifted a hand in greeting to one of the locals who was strolling along the quay. 'It's busy out there today. Day-trippers as well as the usual tourists. The lifeguards are going to be busy on the beach. Let's hope it's a quiet one. There's a wind blowing so I wouldn't be surprised if the lifeboat sees some business today.'

Kyla's fingers drummed on the table. 'She met lots of people.' She emphasised each word carefully, as if English wasn't his first language.

Logan dragged his eyes from the window, obviously alerted by something in his sister's tone. 'Who did?'

'Evanna. On her course on the mainland, she *met lots of people.*'

Evanna blushed. 'Kyla...'

But Kyla was still looking at her brother, a dangerous light in blue eyes that were exactly like his. 'She's been away for a month, remember?'

'You're moody today. Of course I remember.' Logan buttered the second piece of toast. 'Why wouldn't I? We've all been covering her clinics because the agency nurse they sent was hopeless. As I said, it's good to have you back, Evanna.'

Kyla gritted her teeth. 'She went out a lot. Met a lovely registrar. Really nice guy. Good-looking. They got on brilliantly.'

'That's good to hear.' Logan finished his toast, licked his

fingers and rose to his feet, his eyes on the street. 'There's Doug McDonald. Excuse me. I've been trying to catch up with him all week. Since he had the heart attack he's afraid to push himself and I think he needs to do more. Perhaps he could go to your exercise class, Evanna? People always seem to like doing that. I suppose they have confidence because the instructor is a nurse. See you in surgery this afternoon. Janet's booked you a full clinic.' He patted her arm and walked towards the door, pausing by a table to exchange a few words with the couple that ran a small guesthouse near one of the island's best beaches.

'You see?' Evanna's voice was soft and she blinked several times to clear her vision. 'I'm just a piece of medical equipment. His practice nurse. He feels the same way about me as he does about the ECG machine. We're both useful tools that help his life run smoothly. If he could, he'd plug me into the electricity supply to make me function more efficiently.'

Kyla was simmering with frustration. 'I'm starting to think my brother is thick.'

'He isn't thick. He's very clever, you know that. He just isn't interested and that's fine.'

'It isn't fine. How can you say that it's fine?'

Because it had to be. What choice did she have? 'You can't make someone love you, Kyla,' Evanna muttered, reaching down to pick up her bag. Suddenly she just wanted to go home. Back to the peace and tranquillity of her little cottage. She needed to get her thoughts back together before she started work. *Needed to rediscover some of the strength and resolve she'd found during her time on the mainland.*

She dropped some money on the table for her coffee just as the door opened and Fraser stood there, his hat askew and his face scarlet. *'Dr MacNeil!'* He was breathless from running. 'I saw— You have to come—*now.*' He snatched in another tortured breath and Logan turned swiftly, concern in his eyes.

'Fraser? What did you see?' He strode over to the boy and put a hand on his shoulder. 'You must have run like the wind to be this out of breath. It's all right. Calm down. Now, what's happened?'

Fraser waved a hand towards the beach beyond the harbour. 'Drowning.' He sucked in a breath. 'Kid in a rubber dinghy thing. Fell in.'

Without wasting time on questions, Logan left the café at a run with Fraser at his heels.

Evanna and Kyla followed, dodging the throngs of tourists ambling along the quay before sprinting down the steps onto the sand.

'He's gone!' A young woman holding a tiny baby was running up and down the sand at the edge of the waves, frantically scanning the water. 'He was in the boat and now he's gone!'

'I saw him.' Fraser backed away from the mother and moved closer to Logan, instinctively seeking protection from the woman's mounting hysteria and the baby's howling. 'We were up on the cliffs. He leant out of the boat with this bucket thing and a wave caught the boat and he fell. Straight down.'

The woman's wails turned to screams and Logan took Fraser to one side, his tone urgent.

'Where, exactly?' He was ripping off his shirt as he spoke. 'And how long ago did he fall?'

Fraser shrugged. 'About two minutes? We started running down as soon as it happened. The wind's blowing off shore so I suppose it was probably there.' Fraser pointed. 'You want me to go in and look?'

'No. I want you to stay right here.' Logan thrust his clothes into Fraser's hands and handed him a mobile phone. 'Call the coastguard on that and then go to my car and get my bag. Here are the keys. Then stay here with Evanna and do everything she says. Everything.'

'OK.' Fraser nodded importantly and punched the number into the phone. 'I'll give them the details. Be careful, Dr MacNeil.'

Logan looked at Evanna, his ice-blue eyes sharp and alert. 'Beach duty.'

She nodded, reading his mind. He wanted her to coordinate efforts on the beach. He didn't want any of the tourists plunging into the waves on a rescue mission, because they were likely to get into trouble. *He didn't want little Fraser going in.* He wanted her to give support to the mother and then help the rescue services.

Logan lifted the buoyancy aid that he'd grabbed from the top of the beach and ran with a long-limbed, athletic stride towards the sea. At any other time she would have admired the strength and power of his body but the crisis was unfolding in front of her. The mother was screaming now, a thin, high-pitched panicky noise that cut through the air like a knife. A crowd had gathered in the way that humans always gathered when they scented disaster.

Kyla moved them back. 'Come on, now. Nothing to see.' Her tone was clipped. Efficient. 'Move right back, please. Go to the far end of the beach. Right back. That's right. We're going to need to land a helicopter here.'

Fraser was speaking to the coastguard on the phone and Evanna turned to the mother and slid an arm round her shoulders.

'You poor thing. You must be frantic with worry but try and calm down so that we can ask you some questions,' she said gently. 'How old is he?'

'Six.' The mother gave a gulp and jiggled the baby to try and soothe it. 'He's just six. Jason. He's so little.'

'And he was in some sort of boat?'

'I only turned my back for a minute. I was changing the baby.' She sucked air in and out of her lungs, her eyes wild. 'It was just a minute.'

And a minute was more than long enough when water was

involved, Evanna thought as she squinted towards the sea. 'What boat?' She couldn't see a boat. Only a small toy blow-up boat of the sort that people used in swimming pools.

'There! That's it.' The mother pointed to the toy. 'We bought it in the beach shop on the quay.'

'He was in that?' Evanna couldn't quite believe that anyone would have considered such a flimsy toy sufficient protection for a child in open water and her shock must have sounded in her voice because the woman stiffened defensively.

'He was just playing near the shore. I thought he was fine. It was just for a minute...' The woman was sobbing again, clutching at Evanna who supported her and glanced towards Fraser with a question in her eyes.

He slipped Logan's phone into the pocket of his jeans and gave her a thumbs-up.

Evanna smiled her approval and watched as he sprinted across the sand, arms and legs pumping as he went to fetch Logan's bag. 'The lifeboat is on its way.'

The baby was red in the face from howling and Evanna glanced towards Kyla. She gave a nod and strode up to the woman.

'Let me take the baby,' she offered briskly. 'One less thing for you to worry about.'

'I don't want to let her out of my sight.'

'Kyla is a nurse at the local practice,' Evanna said quickly. 'We both are.'

'Oh—in that case, I know I'm just upsetting her.' Struggling with her own sobs, the woman handed the baby over and Kyla expertly tucked the squalling child against her shoulder and walked away.

Evanna calmed the woman as best she could and watched as Logan dived into the waves. He cut through the water with a powerful front crawl, reached the little boat and then made a guess as to where the boy might have fallen.

'Wow.' Fraser was standing beside her, Logan's bag at his feet, his eyes wide with hero-worship as he stared. 'Dr MacNeil must be diving down to look below the surface. He's a brilliant swimmer, isn't he, Nurse Duncan? He got a bronze Olympic medal, didn't he? And he saved that kid two summers ago and it was *all* over the papers. I'm going to be a lifeguard when I'm older, like he was. And a doctor. He's so cool.'

Evanna tried to look relaxed but the tension gripped her like a vice. 'He's a good swimmer, Fraser,' she agreed, as much to reassure herself as the little boy and the mother.

The woman was clutching Evanna's hand. 'We had a terrible night,' she whispered. 'The baby cries all the time and my husband and I are both exhausted so I said I'd bring them both down to the beach for an hour to give him a chance to catch up on some sleep. When Jason asked if he could take the boat in the sea, I didn't even think it would be dangerous. I imagined he'd just stay by the shore.'

'It shelves quite deeply here and the currents are strong,' Fraser said solemnly, and Evanna saw the woman's face pale. And then noticed something.

'There. Can you see the lifeboat?' She lifted a hand and pointed. 'They'll be able to help in the search.'

'But if he's at the bottom of the ocean...' The woman choked on the words.

Then Logan's head bobbed above the water for a few seconds before he disappeared again, this time further out to sea.

Three times his head appeared and then disappeared and on the fourth occasion he came up holding the body of the little boy.

'He's got him. Cool.' Fraser's voice was triumphant but Evanna saw what the mother immediately saw. *That the little boy was limp and lifeless.*

'Spread out your rug,' Evanna ordered. 'Dr MacNeil is going to need somewhere to put him. And get all the layers you can find.'

'It's August.' The woman looked at her blankly and Evanna saw the shock in her eyes.

'It doesn't make any difference that it's August. The sea is still freezing and we're going to need to warm him up. Fraser.' Evanna looked at the boy. 'You and your friends clear a spot for the helicopter to land. You know the drill. Everyone to secure everything that moves. Go. *Move.*'

But she spoke the last few words to the air because Fraser had already sprinted off to do what needed to be done.

Logan strode out of the water, carrying the boy level in his arms. 'I'm going to try tipping him upside down.' His expression was grim. 'He was stuck on the bottom. He must have caught his foot in seaweed. It took me several goes to free him.'

'No!' The mother was screaming with horror and another holidaymaker took her to one side and put her arms around her, giving the medical team space to work.

'Evanna?' Logan's voice was sharp as he laid the boy flat on the rug. 'Did you get my stuff from the car?'

'Fraser did. It's all here.' She flipped open the case. 'His name is Jason and he's six years old. Do you want to start CPR?'

'Not yet.' Logan felt for a carotid pulse. 'I'm hoping he's just bradycardic. Come on, Jason. Wake up, for us. Damn. He's in respiratory arrest.'

'Logan—'

'Respiratory arrest precedes cardiac arrest in drowning. He's got a pulse.' Logan started to examine the boy more thoroughly, his hands swift and skilled. 'Did Fraser manage to bring the oxygen?'

'It's here.'

There was a clacking sound overhead as the helicopter arrived but Logan was focused on Jason, leaving others to deal with the arrival of the helicopter. 'He's breathing but his core temperature is thirty-four degrees. We need to warm him up. What layers do we have?'

Evanna reached forward and covered the boy, noticing that his face was chalky white. 'Do you want to aspirate his stomach?'

Just then the boy screwed up his face and started to cough violently, and Logan gave Evanna a swift nod. 'We have lift-off. Jason? Speak to me. You're worrying your mother. Wake up.'

The boy's eyes fluttered open and he started to cough again.

Logan turned him into the recovery position. 'Good boy. You're all right. You've swallowed a bit of seawater but you'll soon be feeling better. Evanna, this oxygen mask doesn't fit properly. I need something smaller.'

The paramedic from the helicopter sprinted across to them with a case of equipment. 'How's he doing?'

Logan wiped a forearm across his forehead. 'Better than we could have hoped. He's breathing but he's very cold still and he seems to have aspirated water so he'll need to go to hospital for a check.'

The mother sank onto the sand beside Jason, tears pouring down her cheeks. 'He needs to go to hospital? Can't you just watch him here?'

'This is a small island,' Logan said gently, 'and while we are capable of dealing with dire emergencies if the need arises, we do try and anticipate and avoid them whenever possible. I'm sure Jason is going to make an uneventful recovery but, to be on the safe side, I'd rather he made that recovery in the hospital. I'm sure they'll only keep him in for a night.'

'They have rooms for parents,' Evanna said quickly as she found a smaller oxygen mask, 'so you can be with him the whole time.'

'I can go with him in the helicopter?'

The paramedic helped switch masks. 'Of course, but you can't bring the baby.'

'I can leave her with my husband. He'll be fine with her for a day, although the crying will probably drive him mad. We're in one of the beach houses just up there.'

'Go and give the baby to your husband and then you can come with us.' The paramedic squatted down beside Logan. 'Do you want to get a line in just to be on the safe side?'

'Yes, ideally, although he's so cold it's going to be pretty hard getting in a peripheral line.' Logan picked up one of the boy's arms and rubbed the skin. 'We might be lucky.'

With a last, frightened look towards Jason, the mother sprinted across the beach to Kyla who was still holding the baby. Kyla's husband Ethan, the other island GP, arrived and immediately took in the situation. 'You've had one trip to the mainland already today. I'll take this one, Logan.'

'I wouldn't mind, if that's all right with you.' Logan slid the needle into the vein and gave a nod of satisfaction. 'Good. Tape it firmly, Evanna. I don't want to have to try that again.'

Ethan went to supervise the helicopter landing and Kyla turned her attention to the mother.

'His colour is better.' Logan checked the child's pulse again.

'We're ready to transfer him.' Ethan arrived with a stretcher and they carefully lifted the boy, covered him with blankets and secured him. 'You'd better give me a handover.'

Leaving the paramedics to transfer the child into the helicopter, Logan pulled his colleague to one side, told him what had happened and detailed the first aid they'd given.

Watching the helicopter take off, Evanna suddenly realised that her legs were shaking. 'What a day. I think I've aged twenty years and I've only been back on the island for ten minutes!'

Logan sat down next to her. 'I only came down to the quay because I was trying to accidentally on purpose bump into Doug McDonald. I wanted to see how he was doing without looking too obvious.'

'If you hadn't been in the café, the child would have drowned. You were amazing.'

He brushed some sand from his legs and pulled his shirt back on. 'I was doing my job, Evanna. Stop making me sound like some sort of hero.'

'First aid for a drowning incident, that's your job, but going into that water to save a child?' Evanna's voice was soft. 'That's not your job, Logan.'

But he'd do it anyway because that was the sort of man he was.

Logan stood up and pulled on his trousers. 'Fraser was the one who saved the boy. If he hadn't had his eyes open and acted swiftly we would never have found Jason in time.' He lifted a hand and the boy came running over.

'Dr MacNeil. I did everything you said.'

Logan put a hand on his shoulder. 'You're a hero, Fraser.' His voice was gruff. 'You kept a clear head and you didn't panic.'

'You never panic.'

'I'm thirty-one years old. You're twelve.'

Fraser shrugged. 'Bet you didn't panic when you were twelve either. Will that boy be all right? Is he going to die, Dr MacNeil?'

'Thanks to you, I don't think he's going to die.' Logan ran a hand through the boy's hair. 'How's that scar of yours?'

Fraser grinned. 'Wicked. The girls all want to look at it.'

Logan winked and grinned at him, man to man. 'Then let them look. See you around, Fraser.'

'Yeah.' Fraser hooked his fingers in the waistband of his oversized surf shorts and scuffed a foot across the sand. 'The boys and I are going up to the ruins this afternoon. Just to look.'

'Well don't go falling into the dungeons.' Logan watched him go and gave a shake of his head. 'He's growing up.'

'Aisla will be so proud of him.' Evanna stood up, wiped her damp hands down her shorts and started gathering up their equipment. 'I ought to be going. I've got a surgery this afternoon and I haven't even been home yet. My luggage is still in my boot.'

He turned to look at her, his blue eyes searching. 'It's good to have you back. You're always good in a crisis.'

Evanna blushed slightly. And that was how he saw her, of course. Sensible, practical Evanna. Good-in-a-crisis Evanna. What would he say, she wondered, if she told him that she didn't want to be good in a crisis? She didn't want to be sensible, practical Evanna. For once in her life she wanted to be someone's hot fantasy.

She wanted to be *his* hot fantasy.

CHAPTER TWO

THE road clung to the coast, winding high above tiny bays that were accessible only by foot, bays that had once been fiercely defended against Viking invasion. Evanna drove carefully, alert for tourists too busy admiring the view to watch the road. To her right she could see the ruins of the castle where young Fraser had found himself trapped earlier in the summer. To her left was the sparkling ocean, waves crashing onto jagged rocks and, in the distance, the outline of the mainland.

There was nowhere like Glenmore, but today the excitement of being home was missing and she felt frustrated and cross with herself. *And disappointed.* She'd spent a month lecturing herself about the futility of being in love with Dr Logan MacNeil and she'd genuinely thought that finally she had her feelings under control, so the intensity of her reaction in the café was disheartening.

She'd wanted so badly to feel indifferent.

Her spirits lifted slightly as she parked outside her little white cottage with its blue shutters and views of the sea. Buying it had stretched her budget to snapping point but there was never a single moment when she regretted the extravagance. As a child she'd walked past the same cottage with her parents and had stared in wonder. To her it had always looked like the gingerbread house from the fairy tale. Roses clustered around the door and snaked under the windows. It was a friendly house and the fact that it was small had never bothered her. It was hers. And she'd made it her home.

She'd thrown cheerful rugs onto the polished wooden floors, hung filmy white curtains from the windows and filled tall vases with flowers from the garden and glass bowls with shells that she'd found on the beach. And if the second bedroom was so tiny there was barely room for a bed, did it really matter? All the people she knew lived on the island anyway, so she rarely had to find room for overnight guests. Her own bedroom was large enough, and that was what counted. Light streamed through the window and she'd placed the bed so that the first thing she saw when she opened her eyes was the sea. It was a perfect place to sleep, dream and wake up. A room built for lovers.

It was just a shame that she didn't have a lover.

Letting herself into her cottage, Evanna picked up a pile of post and walked into the sunny yellow kitchen that she'd painted herself over a gloomy February weekend earlier in the year. Usually the view from the window across the cliffs cheered her up but today she found it hard to smile.

Telling herself off for being pathetic, she sifted through her post, binning all the junk mail and putting the bills neatly to one side. Then she opened a white envelope and found a quote for redoing her bathroom.

Suddenly resolute, she picked up the phone. 'Craig? Evanna here. About your quote…'

Five minutes later she'd confirmed it all and written out a cheque for the down payment. It would be wonderfully indulgent to have a new bathroom and it was long overdue. The bathroom was the only room that hadn't been touched since she'd bought the cottage three years earlier. It would use the last of her savings but she decided that it was worth it.

Resolving to throw open all the doors and windows at the weekend to freshen the place, Evanna showered, changed and then climbed back into her little car and made her way to the surgery in time for her afternoon surgery.

'I gather you had a drama on the beach. You've a big list, Evanna.' Janet, the receptionist, handed her a computer printout and a pile of letters. 'Plenty of people have been holding on, waiting to see you. And Lucy wanted to know if you could call on your way home to check on the baby because the cord is looking a bit sticky and she's worried. You can tell it's her first. Every time the little one blinks, she rings Logan. He's incredibly patient with her.'

Logan was patient with everyone. 'I'll call, of course I will. I was going to anyway.'

'Who do I have first?'

'Sandra King. She's sitting in the waiting room with a dopey look on her face so I think we all know the reason for her appointment.' Janet winked and Evanna thought back to Kyla's comment.

'Let's hope so. Is she first?'

'Yes.' Janet leaned forward and lowered her voice. 'I made it a double appointment, just to be on the safe side. I had one of my feelings. If I'm wrong, you can use the time to catch up on some of the paperwork that your replacement didn't touch.'

'Good thinking.' Evanna walked through to her room and sat down at her desk. It felt good to be back. She turned her head and glanced around the room. In the corner was a basket stuffed with toys that she'd selected herself and the walls were covered in posters that she'd chosen from the wide selection available to her. Everything was just as she'd left it. The heaviness that had settled inside her lifted and she switched on her computer and pressed the buzzer.

Sandra tapped on the door a few seconds later, her husband by her side. 'I'm pregnant, Nurse Duncan.' She was bursting to tell the news, her smile dominating her pretty face. 'I missed a period and I did the test yesterday and it was positive.'

Full marks to Kyla for observation, then. 'That's great, Sandra. Congratulations.'

'I couldn't sleep at all last night, just thinking about it. I want to have it here, on the Island, and I want you to deliver it,' Sandra blurted out, and Evanna gave a careful smile.

'Why would you want to have him, or her, at home?'

'Because I was born on Glenmore and I want the same for my children.'

'You were the third child,' Evanna said evenly, opening her drawer and pulling out the appropriate forms. 'First babies are better born in hospital, Sandra. I can quite understand your wish for the delivery to be as natural as possible, but we can achieve that in hospital.'

'But I'm young and healthy. Is it because it makes more work for you?'

'It isn't the work for me that's a problem. I love the home deliveries. But having a baby at home does come with risks,' Evanna said, her voice level. 'No obstetrician would ever advise a woman to have her first baby at home. And the other problem is that Glenmore is quite remote. No matter how carefully we monitor you, things can change very quickly in childbirth. Emergencies do happen and when they do, you want to be within easy reach of a specialist unit.'

'But there's the helicopter.'

The memories came rushing back. The evil weather. *Catherine critically ill.* 'If the weather is bad, it can't fly,' Evanna reminded her gruffly, and Sandra was silent for a moment.

'I'm sorry. I didn't think. You're thinking about what happened to Dr MacNeil's wife, aren't you? When Catherine became ill they wanted to fly her to the mainland but the helicopter couldn't get here. She died because of it.'

And Logan, griefstricken and racked by guilt, had made a heroic effort to save the baby.

His daughter. Little Kirsty, now a bouncy, healthy one-year-old.

Evanna felt sadness swamp her but kept her expression neutral. This wasn't the time to think about Logan. 'Catherine MacNeil was an extremely unusual case. It's unlikely that the outcome would have been different, even if she'd been in a consultant unit on the mainland.'

'But we all know that's why Dr MacNeil won't consider home births.' Sandra sighed and glanced at her husband. 'I hadn't really thought about it properly. Perhaps it would be more sensible to have it in hospital. What do you think?'

Her husband nodded, visibly relieved by her change of heart. 'Definitely. You know that was always my preference.'

'The community unit is lovely. I just spent a week there as part of my refresher course,' Evanna told them. 'I did three weeks on the labour ward in the hospital and a week at the unit. They've done up their delivery rooms to look like bedrooms so it's home away from home, really. I think you'll like it.'

'But I can have most of my care with you and Dr MacNeil?'

Evanna nodded. 'Absolutely.'

'Will I need to go to the hospital at all?'

'You'll need to go to there for an ultrasound scan between ten and thirteen weeks,' Evanna told her, reaching for a leaflet, 'and then again between eighteen and twenty weeks for another scan. Apart from that, providing there are no problems, we can do everything else here. Today I'll take some blood from you so that we can check your blood group and screen you for some conditions.'

She ran through all the tests that could be done and Sandra looked at her husband.

'We want all of it, don't we? I'm not taking any chances. You know how long we've waited for this to happen.'

'Can you step on the scales for me, Sandra?' Evanna stood up and reached for some blood bottles. 'I'll just weigh you and check your blood pressure and then I'll take the blood. You can make an appointment with Dr MacNeil to discuss the results and he can listen to your heart and lungs and that sort of thing.'

'I don't even dare look at how much I weigh. Mind you, I've been feeling so sick that I've stopped eating so that might help.' Sandra closed her eyes tightly and pulled a face. 'Is it awful?'

'No.' Evanna scribbled the number on a pad ready to input into the computer. 'Have you actually been sick?'

'Oh, yes.' Sandra stepped off the scales and slipped her shoes back on. 'The moment I wake up I just need to dash to the bathroom. It's awful.'

'Try eating a dry biscuit before you move in the morning.' Evanna checked her blood pressure and recorded the result. 'That's fine. Now, I'll just take that blood sample and you can do me a urine sample and then we'll leave you in peace for a while! Let me give you a pack of information that you can flick through when you have a moment.'

'Is it still all right for me to use the gym?'

'Absolutely.' Evanna took a pack out of her desk and handed it to Sandra. 'It's important to stay fit and active. You're not ill, you're pregnant.'

Sandra smiled. 'I know. And it feels fantastic. I don't even care about the sickness, I'm so excited.'

'It's normal to feel sick in the first few months of pregnancy but we'll keep an eye on the sickness. Let me know if it gets worse. Make an appointment to see Dr MacNeil and another to see me next week. That way, if you have any questions from what you've read, we'll have plenty of time to go over it. I'll send the forms through to the hospital and they'll contact you about the scan. They always try and give islanders a late morning or early afternoon appointment so you have time to get the first ferry out and the last ferry home.'

'Thanks, Nurse Duncan.' Sandra virtually floated out of the room and Evanna watched her go with a wistful smile.

What would it be like, she wondered, *to know that you had a new life growing inside you?*

Giving herself a mental shake, she stood up and walked into Logan's room. 'I've just seen Sandra. She's pregnant and she'll be making an appointment to see you for a check-up.'

Logan had his eyes fixed to the computer screen. 'Tell me you talked her out of having a home birth.'

'I talked her out of it. How did you know she was even thinking about it?'

'I heard a rumour in the pub.' His long fingers tapped several keys and the printer whirred. 'Why does everyone around here seem to be pregnant?'

'Because it's a natural consequence of relationships?' Evanna kept her voice steady. 'I've put all Sandra's observations onto the computer so it should be easy enough to just add in the results of your examination.'

'Thanks. Ethan just rang from the hospital. They've admitted Jason to keep an eye on him.'

'I can't believe she let a six-year-old go out into the Atlantic in a blow-up boat.' Evanna shuddered as she thought of what might have happened. 'Why do people leave their brains behind when they go on holiday?'

'I don't know.' Logan rubbed a hand over the back of his neck. 'That beach is clearly marked as unsafe for inflatable boats but perhaps she didn't see the sign.'

'The baby is obviously wearing them out.' Evanna thought

about what the woman had said. 'I might call later in the week and check on them. I hope Jason is going to be all right. I dread to think how long he was under the water for.'

'Hypothermia can actually give some protection against hypoxia. There have been cases of children recovering after being submerged in cold water for more than forty minutes.' Logan shrugged. 'Once the core temperature drops below thirty-two degrees Celsius, the brain needs less oxygen. Because children get cold very quickly, generally much faster than adults, they might reach that low core temperature before damage occurs from lack of oxygen.'

'But presumably you're worried or you wouldn't have called for the helicopter.'

'There can be late complications, obviously, which is why we transferred him to hospital, just to be on the safe side.' Logan stood up. 'But on the whole the prognosis is reasonable. He was submerged for less than ten minutes, he's young and his core temperature was thirty-four. On the downside, all the signs were that he did aspirate seawater, so they'll need to keep an eye on him until they're sure he's all right. They're going to miss a few days of their holiday.'

'In the circumstances, they're lucky that's all that they're missing.'

'Evanna, about Saturday...' Logan glanced towards her. 'Kyla and I are having a barbecue in your honour. Usual crowd. Six o'clock, my place. We're starting early so that Kirsty can join in. Is that all right with you?'

Evanna's heart lifted and then sank. She should say no. Hadn't she promised herself that she wasn't going to spend so much time with him? It was bad enough seeing him at work, without seeing him socially. But to refuse would look odd because they always socialised in a big group. She just had to adjust her own attitude. She had to try to look at him differently. 'I— That will be lovely.'

'What's the matter?' His eyes searched her face. 'You don't seem your usual cheerful self.'

What could she possibly say to that?

She could hardly confess that she was trying not to be herself because she badly needed to stop loving him! At the moment she would have happily become someone entirely different. Not that that would necessarily help, she thought gloomily, because half the women on the island were in love with Logan MacNeil. The other half was either too old or happily married.

He was perceptive, she acknowledged, about absolutely everything except her feelings for him. And perhaps that was just as well. She didn't really want him knowing how she felt. It would damage their friendship and make things too awkward.

'I'm fine, Logan.' She kept her tone light. 'Just a bit tired after the drive.'

He was still watching her. 'It's probably being in the city. It's far more exhausting than living here, on the island. Well, get some rest before Saturday. Meg, Kyla and a bunch of the cousins are going to be there and I know they'll be disappointed if you don't make it. And Kirsty has really missed you. You have a way with her that no one else has.'

What about you, Logan? she wanted to ask. *Did you miss me, too?* Instead, she smiled through stiff lips. 'In that case, I'll try and be there.' She left the room and bumped into Kyla, who grabbed her wrist and dragged her into the treatment room.

'You look as though you've just been to the dentist for root-canal treatment. What's wrong?'

Evanna told her and then gave a wan smile. 'What am I supposed to do? If I avoid him then I also avoid all the people I love, like Kirsty, you, Meg—your cousins—' She broke off and chewed her lip. 'That's the trouble. I promised myself that I was going to spend less time with him but if I do that then I don't have a social life.'

'It would be much simpler if he just realised that he loved you,' Kyla said gruffly, resting her hips on the couch. 'I've come up with plan B. Plan A, which was for you to forget about him, obviously isn't going to work. So plan B is to make him notice *you*. Once he notices you, he'll realise that he's been in love with you all his life.'

'He married Catherine. He was in love with Catherine.'

'Maybe. But life moves on and I also know that you're perfect for him.'

'Don't start that again.' Evanna started to turn away but Kyla grabbed her arm.

'Just hear me out.' Kyla's voice was urgent. 'I think one of the problems is that you grew up with Logan. You've been my best friend for ever and he's used to seeing you around. He sees you as my friend. His practice nurse. So we need to change all that.'

'And how are we going to do that?'

Kyla grinned. 'Operation makeover. Don't be offended. You're already stunning, it's just that we need to make your charms a little more obvious, so that my thick brother sits up and takes notice of something other than your skill with his patients.'

'What do you want me to do?' Despite her love for her friend, Evanna found it hard to keep the exasperation out of her voice. 'Strap a sign to my body?'

'Figuratively speaking.' Kyla tilted her head to one side. 'Fancy a shopping trip after work tomorrow? Alison has some really nice dresses in the boutique and she's open until eight in the summer. We could grab an early supper in the café afterwards. It would be fun.'

Evanna thought of her mortgage. *Of her new bathroom.* 'I already have a perfectly good wardrobe.'

'But whenever you meet up with my brother you're either in uniform, because you're working, or you're in jeans, because you're looking after Kirsty. That red top looked fabulous on you, but let's make it a red dress.'

'I wear jeans because they're practical.'

'True. But how about forgetting the practical for once and going for the glamorous?'

Evanna stared at her. 'If I turn up to babysit Kirsty in a tiara and diamonds, Logan will have me locked up.'

'Saturday isn't about babysitting. It's a party and I'm not talking about a tiara and diamonds, just something more sexy and frivolous than you would normally wear. Let's just try it. Anyway, shopping is always fun. I'll pick you up from your house.'

'Kyla—'

'Just try it, and then if Logan still doesn't notice you, I'll back off.'

'He won't notice me,' Evanna said flatly. 'It wouldn't matter if I turned up to the barbecue stark naked. He still wouldn't notice me.'

'Trust me,' Kyla said smugly. 'He's going to notice you.'

Evanna dropped in to check on Lucy on her way home from the surgery and was pleased to see her outside in the garden with the pram.

'I thought she might enjoy being out of doors,' Lucy explained as she walked up the path to meet Evanna. 'I've kept her in the shade but she's been crying a bit and being pushed around seems to soothe her.'

'It often does and I quite agree that taking her outside is a good idea. Janet said you're worried about her cord.'

Lucy pulled a face. 'It looks a bit gooey. Do you mind taking a look?'

'Of course not. That's why I'm here. And I'd like to take a look at you, too. How have you been feeling?'

'Excited. Nervous. Being a mum is scary. Knowing that I'm completely responsible for her keeps me awake at night.' Lucy carefully lifted the baby out of the pram. 'Her eyes are a bit sticky, too. Logan gave me some gauze and told me to use that and boiled water to clean them.'

'That sounds like a good strategy. Let's go inside so that I can have a proper look at her.'

'It's so hot today, I've had all the doors and windows open because none of us can sleep at night. I'm really worried that the baby will overheat.'

'Lay her on her back and keep the window open a crack,' Evanna advised, carefully placing the baby on the couch and undoing the poppers on her vest. 'Hello, you gorgeous thing. Can I look at your tummy?' She spoke softly to the baby and Lucy sighed.

'You're so confident when you handle her. I wish I was like that. I'm all fingers and thumbs and I'm terrified that I'm going to drop her or do something wrong. I feel completely ignorant.'

Evanna's eyes slid to the stack of baby books on the coffee-table and she suppressed a smile. 'You're not ignorant, Lucy,' she murmured, turning the nappy down, 'just naturally apprehensive. Mothers should be mothers.'

'I keep ringing Logan,' Lucy confessed. 'Any day now he's going to scream at me for bothering him with trivia.'

'Logan's never yelled at a worried patient in his life. Her cord looks fine, Lucy. Just keep cleaning it the way I showed you in hospital.'

'It isn't infected?'

'No. But try to fold the nappy over so that it doesn't rub.'

'She's so tiny the nappies swamp her.'

Evanna smiled and closed the poppers on the little vest. 'She'll soon grow. How's the feeding going? Are you feeding her yourself?'

'Yes. I really wanted to, you know that. It's hurting quite a bit, though.'

'Is she latching on properly?'

'I suppose so. I don't know really. We're both amateurs.' Lucy gave a helpless shrug. 'She's due a feed now. Could you watch and tell me if we're doing it right?'

'Of course. You make yourself comfortable and I'll go and fetch you a drink of water. It's important to drink plenty when you're feeding, especially when the weather is as hot as it is today.'

Evanna walked through to the kitchen, fetched a glass of water and returned to the sitting room.

'I'm trying to start on a different side each time, like you told me. Ouch.' Lucy winced as the baby's mouth closed over her nipple and Evanna put the glass down on the table and walked over to help.

'She needs more of your breast in her mouth. What's happening is that she's just playing with your nipple, which is why you're getting sore.' Evanna gently repositioned the baby and watched closely as the little jaws clamped down again. 'There. That's better. Does that still hurt?'

'No.' Lucy gave a smile of relief. 'Will you move in with me? I need you here for every feed.'

'You're doing brilliantly. In a few weeks' time this will feel like second nature. Is she doing plenty of wet and dirty nappies?'

'Oh, yes.'

'And are you bleeding much now?'

Lucy shook her head. 'Just spots, you know? Nothing dramatic.'

'Good. We'll just let her finish feeding and then I'll examine you. I want to feel the height of your uterus just to check that it's contracting properly.'

Evanna stayed another hour, answered a non-stop stream of questions from Lucy, satisfied herself that all was well and then finally made her way back to her cottage.

It was hard not to feel envious of Lucy's happiness. Would

it ever be her? *Would she ever be settled with a man that loved her and a baby of her own?*

Reminding herself that she had a great deal to be thankful for, she let herself into her cottage and walked through to her kitchen to make herself supper.

'That one's perfect.' Kyla stood back with her eyes narrowed and Evanna sighed.

'It's too short.' *And too expensive.*

'Too short for what? You have fantastic legs. Stop hiding them under jeans.'

Evanna stared down at herself self-consciously. 'I'm too old for a dress this short.'

'You're twenty-six! And you still look like a teenager. Stop making excuses.' Kyla was laughing as she grabbed a pair of shoes. 'Try these. They'd look great with that dress.'

'I wouldn't be able to walk in them.'

'You don't need to walk,' Kyla said airily, riffling through the rails again and pulling out a scarlet top. 'You can park right outside and just teeter up the path. All you need to do is turn up and look gorgeous. And these would look nice with your jeans on a different occasion so you'll get plenty of wear out of them.'

Evanna gave up arguing and slid her feet into the shoes. 'I'll break my ankle.'

'Don't be so negative. Take a look at yourself in the mirror.'

Evanna stepped forward with a sigh. 'I just don't feel comfortable in anything this short. I'm going to spend my whole evening tugging the—' She broke off as she stared at her reflection. 'Oh.'

'Yes, oh.' Kyla's grin was triumphant as she stretched out a hand and removed the clip from Evanna's hair. 'And you don't need that. Time to let your hair down, Cinderella.'

Evanna's dark curls tumbled over her shoulders. 'I look a mess.'

'You look sexy,' Kyla breathed. 'Incredibly sexy. If Logan doesn't notice you as a woman dressed like that, I'm willing to admit defeat.'

Evanna stared at herself, forced to admit that she did look good. In fact, she looked better than good. The dress skimmed her figure, hinting at curves rather than clinging, and it suited her colouring. She smiled and shook her head. 'This is far too glamorous for a barbecue in the garden.'

'It's perfect. Why are you inventing excuses?'

Evanna was silent for a moment and then she let out a long breath. 'Because I'm scared?' She turned to look at her friend and the smile on her face faltered. 'I'm scared that I'm just setting myself up for yet another knock.'

'You're perfect for each other,' Kyla said softly, all the humour gone from her face. 'Any day now he's going to wake up and realise that.'

Evanna slipped back into the changing room and wriggled out of the dress.

The dress made her feel good. Feminine. But it was an extravagance she couldn't afford.

Wearing her jeans and T-shirt, she stepped out of the changing room with the dress over her arm and the shoes dangling from her fingers. 'It's too expensive, Kyla.'

'It's in the sale.' Alison, who owned the boutique, strolled up to them and named a price that made Evanna stare.

'But it can't possibly be that cheap. I saw the tag.'

'I haven't forgotten what you did for Mum when she was ill,' Alison said gruffly, removing the tag and taking the dress and shoes from Evanna. 'Call it a thank-you from me.'

Evanna was embarrassed. 'You really don't have to—'

'I want to,' Alison said gruffly, folding the dress around tissue paper and sliding it into a bag. 'My mum always said you were an angel. You deserve to look like one.'

CHAPTER THREE

'THIS is an emergency and I have private health care,' boomed a man's voice. 'Just get me a doctor. Call the helicopter or whatever it is you do around these godforsaken parts!'

Evanna heard the commotion in the reception area from her room and hurried out at the same time as Logan.

It was two days after her arrival home and she'd been working non stop to catch up with everything that she'd missed while she'd been away.

The man was looming over the desk, his expression threatening. Sweat beaded on his brow and his stomach bulged against a T-shirt that was too tight. 'We're only here for a week. If I waste a morning, that's a chunk of my holiday gone!'

'Obviously we're doing our best to see everyone,' Janet said smoothly, 'but Dr Walker was called out on an emergency and Dr MacNeil is seeing his patients, too, and that means that—'

'I keep telling you I have private health care! I can pay.' The man pulled a fat wallet out of his back pocket and lifted an eyebrow. 'How much to jump the queue?'

Logan stepped up behind him. 'We don't offer private health care,' he said calmly, his ice-blue eyes narrowed and assessing as he looked at the man. 'Here on Glenmore, it isn't necessary.

People get seen according to need. If there's no urgency, they wait in line.'

'Well, then, you need to organise yourselves a bit better,' the man spluttered, 'because the line is too long!'

'My partner has had to attend a sick patient,' Logan explained, his voice reasonable, 'so I'm running two lists at the moment. We're seeing patients in the order they arrived, unless someone has an urgent condition.'

'That girl—' the man pointed a finger at little Nicola Horsfield, who shrank closer to her mother '—came in after me and she's going in next.'

'Nicola is severely asthmatic and the heat is bothering her. She's six years old. Do you feel that your medical condition requires you to go in front of her?'

Evanna watched from the doorway but not because her presence was needed. *Just because she couldn't help herself.* Logan was such a master at dealing with difficult people that watching him was a pleasure.

He managed to sound pleasant and reasonable while staying in complete control of the situation.

The man frowned. 'It isn't about queue jumping—'

'There's one doctor and a line of people. That's generally called a queue.'

'You could get me a helicopter to the mainland.'

Logan lifted an eyebrow. 'Are you bleeding, suffering severe chest pains or having breathing problems?'

'No, but—'

'Are you in imminent danger of death or collapse?'

'No, but—'

'Then I'm not ordering the helicopter.'

'I'll call it myself.'

'As island doctor, it requires my authorisation.' Logan glanced at his watch. 'In the time I've taken having this discussion, I could have seen another patient. Do you want to carry on talking or would you rather go outside, breathe in some fresh Glenmore air and cool down? Janet will call you when it's your turn.'

The man inhaled sharply, tightened his mouth and then stomped out of the door.

Logan gave Janet an encouraging smile. 'I'm ready for my next patient. If he gives you any more problems, buzz me.'

Janet leaned forward. 'He's only here because he forgot to bring his tablets on holiday. He wants a prescription.'

'People get cross when the weather heats up.' Logan turned away and caught sight of Evanna. 'What are you doing standing there, Nurse Duncan?' His blue eyes gleamed with humour. 'Getting ready to defend me?'

'You don't need any help. But I was ready to pick him up after you floored him.'

'As if.'

She grinned. 'Logan MacNeil, you were always knocking people flat in the school playground. You were always in Ann Carne's office.'

At the mention of their old headmistress, Logan laughed. 'Well, they all deserved it and I wasn't a doctor then. Now I try not to knock people down because it just makes more work.' He strolled back towards his surgery. 'Ethan should be back soon and then we can start clearing everyone from the waiting room.'

Evanna went back into her own consulting room and buzzed for her next patient.

'He almost fell off the quay into the water!' The young mother cuddled the toddler on her lap. 'He gave me a heart attack. My husband was buying ice creams so he didn't even see it happen. I caught him by instinct, but now he isn't using his arm and I'm worried I've done something awful to his wrist.'

Evanna scribbled a note on her pad and then reached for the

fox puppet that she kept on her desk. She slid her hand inside and made the fox move.

The toddler smiled and reached for the puppet. 'Mine.'

'He likes to be stroked,' Evanna murmured, noticing that the toddler favoured one arm. She glanced back at the mother. 'How did you catch him?'

'I caught his wrist and jerked him up to stop him falling.'

'So his weight would have been on his arm?'

'Yes.' The mother bit her lip. 'Have I broken his wrist?'

'From the sound of it, you did what needed to save him from falling into the water. Looking after an inquisitive toddler is never easy,' Evanna said steadily, thinking of the number of times that little Kirsty had surprised her with her antics. She wiggled the fox and smiled at the child. 'Can you stroke foxy with your other hand, William?'

The toddler ignored her request and kept one arm firmly in his lap.

Evanna put the fox down on her desk. 'He obviously doesn't want to use that arm so I think we do need to ask one of the doctors to check him out. I'll just nip across the corridor and see if one of them is free to take a look.'

'You think he's broken his wrist? Oh, no, and we're on holiday here in the middle of nowhere.'

'I think he may have injured his elbow,' Evanna said gently. 'And Glenmore may be remote but we have a surprisingly large population and two excellent doctors who are used to dealing with all sorts of injuries. Try not to worry.'

The red light was showing outside Ethan Walker's consulting room, which meant that he was back from his house call and busy catching up with his patients. She hesitated outside Logan's door, rapped sharply and then entered when she heard his voice. 'Sorry to bother you. I know we've got a backlog, but I've a toddler in my room who looks as though he might have a pulled elbow. His mother caught him by the arm to stop him falling off the quay.'

Logan sat back in his chair. 'You've taken a look at him?'

'He isn't moving the arm.'

'I'll examine him in your room. Ethan's back now anyway, so things are calming down.' He rose to his feet in a fluid, athletic movement and strode across to her, strands of dark hair flopping over his forehead. His skin was bronzed from the summer sun, his eyelashes thick and dark, and Evanna quickly turned and opened the door, trying not to look at him.

She felt awkward and self-conscious in his company and despair rose inside her. Being full of good intentions was one thing, but somehow she had to communicate her new resolve to her body. She needed to stop her knees shaking and her stomach spinning.

'I'm Dr MacNeil.' He shook hands with the parents and then dropped into a crouch and smiled at the little boy. 'What have you been up to, William? Trying to dive off our quay?'

'Fox.'

'You like Evanna's fox, do you?' Logan carefully examined the child's hand, wrist and shoulder. 'There's no obvious swelling. Does this hurt, William?'

'Ow.' The toddler jerked and his face crumpled.

'Obviously the answer to that question is yes. Sorry to hurt you, little chap,' Logan murmured apologetically, stroking a hand over the toddler's head and reaching for the fox puppet. He waggled it around, made the child smile and then glanced at Evanna. 'He's tender over the radiohumeral joint. He's comfortable until you try and move the elbow. It's all consistent with a subluxation of the head of the radius. I'll reduce it here.'

'Here?' The mother tensed. 'Doesn't he need an X-ray or anything?'

'If there was any suspicion of a fracture, I'd arrange for an

X-ray,' Logan said easily, standing up and crossing the room to wash his hands, 'but all the signs are that your son's elbow is slightly out of place and I'm sure I can correct that. It will hurt for a few moments and then hopefully he'll be fine. If this doesn't do the trick, yes, I'll consider an X-ray as the next step.'

Evanna stepped forward. 'Can you hold him on your lap? Like that—perfect.' She settled the child while Logan ripped a paper towel out of the dispenser and dried his hands.

'All right, William, let's do this so that you can get on with your holiday. Have you tried the ice cream at Meg's Café yet?' He put his thumb over the head of the radius and pressed down while he smoothly extended the elbow. 'It's the best ice cream in the world.'

Evanna watched while he moved the arm and then flexed the elbow, keeping his thumb pressing against the radial head.

The toddler screamed loudly and the mother inhaled and covered her mouth with her hand, but Logan gave a satisfied nod.

'Sorry about the pain but I think that should have done the trick. I felt a click against my thumb. I'd like you to hang around here for about ten minutes, if that's all right, then I'll take another look at him.'

'That's it?' The mother was cuddling William but he'd already stopped crying and was watching, fascinated, as Evanna made the fox puppet perform a series of elaborate tricks. 'Does he need a plaster or a sling or anything?'

Logan shook his head. 'I think he's going to be fine. Let him play with the toys in the waiting room and then I'll give you a shout and take another look. Good boy, William. You were very brave.'

The mother let out a sigh of relief. 'I thought I'd broken his wrist.'

'A sudden jerk on the arm can be enough to pull the elbow in a child of this age.'

'I'll remember that. I have a set of reins in the car but he hates them.'

'He'll probably like them more than having me manipulating his arm,' Logan said gently. 'Use them, at least when you're near the water.'

The mother nodded. 'Thanks very much.'

Logan smiled and walked towards the door. 'I'll see you in ten minutes.'

Evanna showed the couple into the waiting room, settled William with some toys and then returned to her room.

It would help if Logan weren't such a good doctor, she thought wearily as she completed her notes and buzzed for her next patient. It would be so much easier if she didn't admire him so much. She needed to work hard at finding something significantly wrong with him.

'Keep the dressing on over the weekend, Mrs Keen,' she said ten minutes later as she secured the bandage and helped the old lady to her feet. 'Make an appointment with Janet to see me on Monday and I'll look at it then, but it's healing nicely.'

'What are you doing this weekend, dear?' The old lady reached for her bag. 'Anything nice?'

Evanna thought of the barbecue and the new dress hanging in her wardrobe. 'I'm not sure. Possibly.' It would probably depend on the outcome of her new outfit. Would Logan notice a difference in her? And would he even care?

She walked Mrs Keen to the waiting room and brought William and his family back to Logan.

'He seems fine now.' The mother was smiling. 'He's using the hand quite happily. I can't quite believe the difference. I was imagining that we were going to have to go back to the mainland for treatment. Thank you so much.'

'You're very welcome.' Logan smiled and checked the child's arm carefully, satisfying himself that an X-ray wasn't necessary. 'I think he's fine, but if there are any more problems just come back to us and we'll take another look. If he seems reluctant to use it, I want to know. Otherwise, enjoy the rest of your holiday! And don't forget to try that ice cream.'

The toddler gave him a faltering smile and Logan ruffled his hair. 'And don't go near the edge of the quay.'

'He almost gave me a heart attack.' The mother smiled her thanks again and left the room.

'Are we nearly done here?' Logan glanced at his watch. 'I want to have lunch with Kirsty. Why don't you join us? You haven't seen her since you arrived back. She misses you.'

Evanna felt something twist inside her.

What should she say? That she was trying to gradually distance herself from his family to make the whole thing easier to live with?

No, to say that would trigger a full confession and she couldn't think of anything more embarrassing. And, anyway, she didn't really want to distance herself from Logan and Kirsty. She enjoyed their company. She just wanted to feel differently about him.

'I've been away for a month, Logan,' she said quietly, picking up two empty mugs from his desk. 'I've had things to do in the cottage.'

'Yes, of course you have.' His gaze was searching. 'It's just that you usually spend a lot of time with Kirsty.'

Oh, what the heck! 'I'd like to see her,' she said weakly, cursing her lack of self-discipline. 'I'll make us all a sandwich.'

After all, what difference was it going to make? She couldn't possibly love Logan more than she did already and she couldn't possibly feel any worse than she did already. So she may as well just make the most of the time she had with him.

'Good.' He was still watching her. 'Are you sure you're all right? You seem a bit…edgy. Is something the matter?'

Yes, Evanna thought to herself as she walked towards the

door, clutching the mugs. *I'm in love with a man who doesn't know I exist.* 'Nothing's the matter. I've finished my clinic so I'll go through to the house and get lunch on the table. Join us whenever you're ready.'

Something was the matter with Evanna.

Frowning to himself, Logan closed the door of his consulting room, handed a pile of letters to Janet and walked through the door that connected with his house.

It was unlike Evanna to be distracted and yet ever since she'd returned from the mainland she seemed really...jumpy?

Perhaps it was his imagination. It was just that he wasn't used to having to wonder about her. Unlike his sister, who wasn't above throwing something at him when he annoyed her, Evanna was always steady and consistent.

In fact, if he'd been asked to find one word to describe Evanna it would have been predictable. Reliable. Kind. That was more than one word, he acknowledged with a faint smile as he followed the sound of laughter and walked into his kitchen.

Evanna was sitting at the huge table, gingerly wiping blobs of strawberry yoghurt from her dark hair. Kirsty was gurgling with delight and banging her spoon on her high chair.

'Yes, yes,' Evanna was saying in that soft, breathy voice that always soothed anxious patients, 'your aim is fantastic.'

'Sorry.' Logan laughed as he walked over to her and handed her some more kitchen roll. 'I should have warned you about her new throwing technique. I think she might be a cricketer when she grows up. She's quite good at bowling food.'

'I noticed.' Evanna leaned forward, undid the harness and lifted the little girl out of her high chair. 'Come on, then, monster. Let's have a cuddle.'

All smiles, Kirsty wrapped her arms round Evanna's neck and kissed her on the cheek.

Logan felt an aching sadness rise up inside him.

'Are you all right?' Evanna stood up, lifting the child onto her hip. 'Logan?'

She was watching him with dark, solemn eyes and he pulled himself together. 'I'm fine.'

'No, you're not.' Her voice was gentle as she sat the toddler down on the floor next to a pile of toys. 'You were thinking about Catherine. You don't have to pretend with me, Logan. You spend most of your life putting on a brave face in public, you're allowed to let it slip when you're with friends.'

She was so astute. She always saw through to the real emotions. It was what made her such an outstanding nurse. It was why everyone on the island loved her. Evanna cared. Deeply.

Wondering why he always talked to Evanna about things that he never usually talked about, Logan stared at his daughter. 'It's just hard not to worry about her. She needs a mother,' he said gruffly, and Evanna walked over to him and touched his arm.

'Kirsty is a lucky girl.' Her voice was husky with emotion. 'She has an amazing father who adores her. Don't underestimate that. You're doing a good job, Logan.'

'Am I?' His expression was bleak and for a moment he felt empty inside. 'I'm not sure that I have the skills to be a mother and a father to a child.'

'Kirsty has plenty of loving females in her life. She's surrounded by family. What with Kyla and all the aunts and cousins—your parents—' Evanna broke off and sighed. 'I'm sorry. I'm trying to make you feel better. Human instinct. The truth is it's a vile situation that no one should ever have to find themselves tackling. Life is hideously unfair. Feel free to scream, swear and complain as much as you like. I'm always here, you know that.'

He did know that. Evanna was rock-solid and dependable. Always there when he needed her.

And she had the lightest of touches when it came to awkward

situations, Logan thought, watching as she turned away to make them both a sandwich. Other people offered empty platitudes or just ignored the subject altogether because it was just too uncomfortable. Evanna never ignored things. She was happy to listen or to talk, depending on his mood. It was one of the reasons he felt so comfortable with her. There were never any awkward moments with Evanna. 'People keep telling me that I'll find someone else. It's just one of the things that people say to you when someone dies. "You'll find someone else." As if people you want to spend a lifetime with are waiting round every corner.' He saw the sudden stillness in her frame.

'I suppose they're just trying to help. People love you and care about you,' she mumbled, keeping her back to him. 'I'm sure that one day you will find someone else, even if it doesn't feel that way now.'

'Do you? Do you really believe that?'

Her hesitation was so brief that he wondered if he'd imagined it. 'Yes. What would you like in your sandwich?'

'Anything. But love doesn't happen that often, does it? Look at you, Evanna. You're beautiful and sweet-natured and you'd make someone an amazing wife, but you're still single.'

Her head was in the fridge so he could barely hear her reply, but he thought she said, 'That's right. I am.'

After what seemed like an age she turned with a bag of salad in her hand. 'This is soggy and horrible.' Her voice sounded strange. 'When did you last shop?'

'Meg filled the fridge last weekend but I've been too busy to do much with it.'

She gave a faint smile of understanding. 'It's always the same in the summer, isn't it? Tourists double the workload and, goodness knows, you work hard enough as it is. I'll do a quick shop for you later and make a couple of casseroles for your freezer.' Evanna dropped the salad in the bin and added a carton of tomatoes and a soft, liquid cucumber. 'This is vile, Logan. Most of the food in your fridge died at least a century ago. You're going to poison yourself and Kirsty.'

'She's OK. She's still eating the stuff you left in the freezer for her and I've lived on take-aways all week,' he confessed, watching absently as she swiftly stripped his fridge of dubious food and tidied the rest neatly. She was so methodical and efficient. 'Or else I go down to Meg's and eat at the café.'

Evanna peered at the date on a packet of ham. 'Miracles do happen. This is still all right.'

'It's so good to have you home. We missed you when you were away,' he said gruffly, and she turned to look at him, a strange light in her eyes.

There was something about the expression on her sweet face that made him uneasy.

Why did he constantly have a niggling feeling that there was something the matter with her?

Logan shook himself mentally and decided that he was imagining things.

Having been away for a month, it was bound to take her a little while to get back into the swing of island life.

'How's it been going with Amy Foster?' She turned back to her sandwich-making. With a minimum of fuss she buttered bread, layered the ham, added a dab of mustard and handed him the sandwich. 'She seems sweet with Kirsty. Is it working out, her helping you out?'

'I've no problem with the way she cares for Kirsty.' Logan bit into the sandwich, wondering how she'd managed to make something so delicious from the limited contents of his fridge.

'But you have a problem with something else?' Evanna sat down opposite him and Logan gave a weary smile.

'Only the usual. She's obviously one of the many people who think that I should get married again. Soon. Preferably to her.'

Evanna cut her sandwich in two. 'Oh, dear.'

'I'm a widower.' Logan rubbed a hand over his brow and then gave a bitter laugh. 'Do you have any idea how much I hate that word? It sounds so pathetic.'

'Pathetic?' Evanna frowned and put the knife down. 'You're the strongest man I know, Logan. And it's natural that women are going to fall for you.'

'Why?' It didn't make sense to him. 'Because I'm single and well off with a child who needs mothering?'

She stared at him for a moment and he had a strong feeling that she was about to say something. Then she blushed slightly and lifted her sandwich. 'I've no idea why.'

'Well, of course you haven't.' He laughed. 'That's why we're such good friends. In fact, I think you're the only woman on this island, apart from my sister and cousins, who hasn't made a pass at me in the last year. Our relationship is wonderfully platonic. Perhaps what I really need is a male nanny. Anyway, I've tactfully fired Amy. I told her that you were back from the mainland and that I wouldn't need the help any more. One of the cousins is going to look after her during the day when Meg is busy at the café, but I worry about Kirsty having so many different carers.'

Evanna nibbled at her sandwich. 'They're mostly family,' she muttered, apparently absorbed by what was on her plate. 'Kirsty will be fine.'

'You're not eating much.'

She put the remains of her sandwich down and stood up. 'I'm not that hungry. I'll clear up here and get back to the surgery because I still have some paperwork to catch up on before the immunisation clinic this afternoon.'

'You've had less than half an hour.' He frowned at her. 'I know we're busy but don't overdo the work, Evanna.'

'It's fine. I'm fine.' She gave a quick smile and backed towards the door.

If he hadn't known better, he would have said that she was anxious to get away from him and he couldn't shake the feeling that something was wrong with her.

Pushing away thoughts of that entirely disturbing conversation over lunch, Evanna tried to concentrate on her work.

Her first patient of the afternoon was Sonia, who was thirty-four weeks pregnant. Evanna noticed that she looked hot and bothered. 'How have you been?'

'All right.' Sonia sank into the chair and rubbed a hand over her swollen abdomen. 'I wish it wasn't so hot. This is Glenmore. We don't normally have heat waves. Suddenly I'm longing for a good old storm to clear the air. I brought you a sample. I assume you wanted one?'

Evanna nodded and took the sample. 'I'll just test this quickly and then check your blood pressure.' She used a dipstick and checked that there was no protein in the sample. Then she checked Sonia's blood pressure. 'That's a bit on the high side, Sonia. Why don't you lie down on the couch and I'll feel the baby and then I'll check it again.'

She skilfully palpated Sonia's bump, feeling the lie of the baby, and then she used her tape measure to check the size. 'Well, that's all as it should be.'

'Apart from the blood pressure.'

'I'm going to try that again now that you've sat down for a few minutes.'

Sonia watched anxiously while she checked it. 'Well?'

'It's still a bit high, Sonia.' Evanna recorded the result. 'I'm going to mention it to Dr MacNeil and I'll pop round to your house on my way home and check it again.'

'Will it be different in my home?' Sonia sat up and wriggled off the trolley.

'It might be.'

Sonia bit her lip. 'Will I have to go to the hospital?'

'I hope not. We certainly need to keep an eye on that blood pressure but there's nothing to worry about so far. Are you feeling plenty of movements?'

Sonia picked up her bag. 'Oh, yes. I'm definitely having a footballer. It kicks and moves all the time.'

Evanna smiled and slipped her pen into her pocket. 'That's good. I'll see you later, Sonia.'

'I'll make sure to have the kettle on.'

Evanna watched her go and then walked across to talk to Logan, who had just finished his afternoon surgery.

'I'm taking Kirsty down to the beach for a paddle. Do you want to come?' His hair was rumpled, his jaw slightly darkened with the beginnings of stubble, and he gave her a sleepy, sexy smile that made her breath catch.

She gazed at him wistfully and then reminded herself that playing happy families was not a good idea. 'Actually I can't,' she said truthfully. 'I have a few things to do here and then I have to call on Sonia.'

'She was just in surgery.' He pushed some papers into his bag and closed it. 'Why would you be calling on her?'

'Because her blood pressure is up a bit. It's one-forty over ninety.'

The smile left his face. 'Did you test her urine?' His voice was terse and Evanna wondered how long it would take him to stop treating pregnant women as if they were unexploded bombs.

'Of course. It was negative and her fundal height measurement was fine—thirty-five centimetres.'

'Is the baby moving around?'

'Yes. Plenty of movement. I've arranged to call with her later to check her blood pressure again, but I just wanted to let you know.'

Logan nodded. 'If her blood pressure is still up, ask her to come to surgery tomorrow so that we can take some blood. We'll do a single estimate serum urate, urea and electrolytes, full blood count and platelets, and repeat blood pressure recording and urinalysis.'

Evanna gave a soft smile. He was the most thorough, dedicated doctor she'd ever worked with. He let nothing slip past him. 'All right.'

'And Evanna—' he picked up the case and walked towards the door '—don't forget about the barbecue on Saturday.'

Evanna thought of the dress in her wardrobe. The *new* dress. 'I won't forget.'

'Good.' He gave a nod of approval and reached for his car keys. 'See you tomorrow.'

Evanna called in at Sonia's on the way home to check on her and found her blood pressure was still slightly high. Evanna felt a flicker of unease as she closed her bag and thought carefully about the best course of action.

'Dr MacNeil wants you to come to surgery tomorrow and have a blood test,' she said as she walked towards the door. 'And can you bring another sample?'

'Of course.' Sonia winced slightly and rubbed her bump. 'I must admit I'm starting to find it quite uncomfortable. It's the heat, I suppose. Next time I'm going to make sure that I'm pregnant in the winter. Glad I'm not having triplets.'

Evanna smiled. 'I'll see you tomorrow, Sonia.'

She climbed back into the car, lining up the facts and deciding on the best course of action. Tests tomorrow and then careful monitoring. And, if in doubt, she'd send Sonia to the hospital for a check. She wouldn't take any chances.

Suddenly she felt excited about Saturday. Maybe Kyla was right. When had she ever really dressed up for Logan? The answer was never. Yes, they sometimes went to social events at the same time, but she'd never dressed to attract his attention.

He obviously liked her company and there was no doubt that Kirsty loved her.

Perhaps it was just a question of showing him that she was interested—of showing him that, as well as his friend and colleague, she was also a woman.

CHAPTER FOUR

SATURDAY evening arrived and Evanna hovered outside Logan's house, feeling ridiculously self-conscious. She'd walked through his garden gate at least a thousand times in her life and never even hesitated. So why should a glamorous dress and a pair of high heels suddenly make her nervous?

The answer, of course, was because she felt…different.

Normally, when she joined Logan for one of the frequent barbecues at his house, she pulled on her oldest pair of jeans and pushed her feet into a pair of trainers. It was true that occasionally she'd worn a dress in the hope that he'd notice her, but it had never worked. *But she'd never worn a dress as glamorous or feminine as the one she was wearing now.*

Lifting a hand to her hair, she drew in a breath and opened the gate.

'Evanna, you look wonderful!' Meg, Kyla's aunt who owned the café on the quay, stepped forward, a drink in her hand. 'I've never seen your hair down like that! It looks amazing.'

'I—I thought I'd have a change from curls.' Evanna's eyes slid nervously around the garden, which was already crowded with Logan's friends and family. 'Where's Kirsty?'

It was ridiculous, she thought to herself, *hiding behind a child.* But suddenly that was what she wanted to do.

'Last seen clinging adoringly to her father, but you don't want to hold her while you're wearing that gorgeous dress. She was squashing raspberries into her mouth a moment ago and most of the juice was stuck to her.'

Evanna laughed. 'She loves fruit.'

'There she is.' Meg smiled benignly across the garden. 'And Logan is looking well, don't you think? That blue shirt with his eyes—it's no wonder the girls all trip over themselves when he passes. He's not going to be on his own for long, that's for sure. Someone is going to snap him up really soon.'

Were they?

Wondering how she'd cope with that, Evanna kept her smile fixed firmly in place, relieved to see Kyla walking across to them, her hand in Ethan's.

'Good to see Kyla so happy, too,' Meg said, nodding approvingly as Ethan paused to kiss his new wife on the lips. 'Ethan may not be an islander born and bred, but you wouldn't know it to look at him. He fits right in.'

Evanna nodded. It was true that Ethan fitted in. He'd arrived as a locum GP to help Logan and had fallen in love with Kyla and stayed. It was a situation that suited everyone. 'He was always meant to come here.'

'You mean because he's Kirsty's uncle?' Meg lowered her voice. 'I must admit I wasn't surprised when he revealed that he was actually related to Logan's late wife. Her brother, imagine! There was always something secretive about him. And about her, come to that. She certainly never mentioned a brother.'

'They weren't close. That's why Ethan took the job here. To try and learn more about her. I'm sure that if she hadn't died, they would have developed a relationship.' Kyla hadn't shared much of it with her, but Evanna knew that Ethan and Catherine had shared a difficult family background.

Meg sniffed. 'Well, he's a good doctor and that's what

matters. Oh, look at that.' She waved a hand. 'Kirsty has spotted you. And Logan.'

Evanna felt her heart rate double. 'I'd better go and say hello.'

'You do that. And watch that dress.'

Evanna caught Kyla's whispered 'Nice cleavage', took a deep breath and plucked up courage to walk across the lawn.

'Hello, Kirsty,' she said, clasping the raspberry-stained fist in hers and giving it a swift kiss. 'No need to ask what you've been eating.'

Kirsty chortled with delight, a huge smile on her plump cheeks.

'I've given up trying to keep her clean,' Logan murmured, dropping a kiss onto his daughter's silken blonde curls. 'It's a losing battle. I've decided that I'm just going to turn the hose onto her before she goes to bed.'

'It's a good job I know you're joking.' Evanna felt her heart hammer against her chest as he turned to look at her. His blue eyes were shielded by thick, dark lashes and her stomach flipped as she fell into that sleepy, masculine gaze.

Suddenly she felt agonisingly nervous.

What if he hated the way she looked? What if he thought she looked ridiculous? What if—?

He smiled at her. 'I'm glad you came early.'

Didn't he notice anything different about her? Evanna shook her head gently, allowing her smooth, shiny hair to spill over her shoulders.

Kirsty gave a delighted gurgle and immediately reached out and grabbed a handful.

'Don't pull Evanna's hair,' Logan drawled, prising the little girl's fists open and giving Evanna an apologetic smile. 'You know what she's like with hair. Leaving it down was asking for trouble. You should have worn it in a ponytail, like you usually do.'

Evanna swallowed back her disappointment.

That was it?

That was all he was going to say?

That she should have worn her hair in a ponytail? 'Yes,' she croaked, 'I probably should.'

Kyla stepped up to them, a bowl of plump, glossy black olives in her hand. 'Olive, anyone? Doesn't Evanna look fantastic with her hair like that, Logan? It's stunning, Evanna. Really stunning. You should wear it down more often.'

'Well, it certainly makes it easier for Kirsty to pull,' Logan said absently, stretching out a hand and helping himself to an olive. 'I'm going to put the baby to bed now. Then I'll come down and cook. Did you know that Meg has offered Fraser free ice creams for the whole of the summer as a reward for his quick reactions last week?'

'That's a bit rash, isn't it? I've seen how much that boy can put away.' Kyla grinned and held out her arms to Kirsty. 'Come to your Aunty Kyla. I'll put her to bed. You chat to Evanna. You two never have time to talk properly and I'm sure you have lots to catch up on.'

Logan looked surprised. 'All right, thanks. But I'm going to talk Evanna into making a salad while I get the barbecue going.'

'Evanna is not making salad while she's wearing that dress,' Kyla said firmly, and Logan frowned slightly.

'She could wear an apron.'

Kyla gritted her teeth. 'Ethan is going to finish off the cooking. You two just spend a bit of time together.' She walked off with the toddler in her arms and Logan watched her go.

'Well, perhaps we should take her up on her offer. To be honest, I was trying to work out a way of getting you on your own before everyone else arrives. This seems like as good a time as any.' He closed a hand on her arm and pulled her across the grass to the weeping willow. Green tentacles spilled downwards, providing shade and privacy.

His touch was firm and purposeful and Evanna felt her heart start to pound. What could he possibly want to say to her?

He pushed aside the soft curtain of leaves and led her into the cool, shaded centre of the tree. Although they were still in the middle of the garden, it felt secluded and private and suddenly Evanna started to shiver. Trapped in such an intimate atmosphere, she was acutely aware of him and she couldn't look away. He was a strong man in every sense and that strength showed in the rugged planes of his handsome face and the easy, confident way he dealt with everyone on the island.

'L-little Jason is d-doing really well,' she stammered. 'I called in to see them in their holiday cottage. The hospital kept him in for a few days and then sent him home so they were able to continue their holiday. I gave them some advice on the baby. I think she was just hot and uncomfortable, that's why she was crying so much. They were putting too many layers on her and not giving her enough fluid.'

'You're a genius.' Logan leaned his shoulders against the wide trunk of the tree. 'It always amazes me how little thought people give to the weather. I stopped the car this morning to tell a couple to put sun cream on their baby.'

'What did they say?'

He grinned. 'I think their comment was, "Who do you think you are?" To which I replied, "The guy you're going to see when she's burnt and miserable."' He lifted his beer to his lips. 'Funnily enough, that seemed to shut them up. I saw them in the shop later, buying sun cream by the bucketload.'

Evanna laughed. She'd always liked that about him. The way he wasn't afraid to speak up when he saw something that he didn't agree with. 'I've never understood why people insist on putting small babies in the sun.'

'Ignorance. I really do need to talk to you,' he drawled softly, lifting a hand and removing a leaf from her hair. 'And I honestly don't know how you're going to react to what I'm going to say. You're probably going to refuse.'

Refuse?

When had she refused him anything?

Her legs were shaking so badly that she stepped backwards and leaned against the broad trunk of the tree for support. 'Just say it, Logan.'

'All right. But if I'm overstepping the bounds of our friendship then I want you to tell me. Do you promise to give me an honest answer?'

Overstepping the bounds of their friendship?

Hope and anticipation made her suddenly dizzy. 'Yes,' she mumbled, her hands fisting by her sides. 'Of course.' The weeping willow provided a lush, delicate screen from the rest of the garden and suddenly the atmosphere seemed impossibly intimate. It was just the two of them, everyone else forgotten.

He took a deep breath. 'I wondered if you'd consider looking after Kirsty for me on Wednesday afternoons. I know it's usually your afternoon off, but it wouldn't be for ever. Just until I find someone to replace Amy Foster.'

Evanna stared at him. The words he'd spoken were so different from the ones she'd longed to hear that it took her a moment from the meaning to sink in. 'You want me to look after Kirsty? That's what you wanted to ask me?'

'Yes. I know it's a lot to ask. You've often looked after her before, but not on a regular basis. Is the answer going to be no?' He strolled towards her, powerfully built and handsome. *The man she'd loved for the whole of her life.*

She looked away for a moment, struggling to compose herself. Then she cleared her throat carefully. 'Logan...' Her voice cracked. 'Can I ask you something?'

'Of course. Anything.'

What do I have to do to make you notice me? 'Why ask me? Why me?'

'Because you're completely reliable, a wonderful cook, incredibly uncomplicated and Kirsty adores you. That's just a start but I could go on for ever.' He gave a shrug and a lopsided smile. 'If I didn't need you in the practice so badly, I'd fire you and employ you to look after Kirsty full time.'

So he was happy for her to care for his daughter.

That was a compliment, of course. But it was so much less than she wanted.

Evanna stood for a moment, thinking of the heat and the passion she saw in Ethan's eyes when he looked at Kyla. Then she looked at Logan. And saw humour and a faint question in his gorgeous blue eyes.

For him, their relationship was all about friendship. Nothing else.

'Evanna?'

She realised that he was waiting for an answer. And how could she refuse? She loved him. She'd loved him all her life. She'd loved him when he'd been a boy at school and she'd loved him when he'd grown into a man and married another woman.

And she loved Kirsty.

How could she refuse to help him? What sort of a friend would that make her? It wasn't Logan's fault that her feelings towards him were entirely more complicated than his were for her.

He deserved all the help she could give him, even if it proved to be torture for her.

With a smile that cost her greatly in terms of effort, she forced the words past her dry lips. 'Of course I'll look after Kirsty on Wednesdays. It would be my pleasure.'

His eyes were on her face. 'I don't expect you to do it for nothing. I'll pay you.'

Employee. Friend. He offered her just about every role

except the one she wanted. 'I don't want to be paid, Logan,' she said quietly. 'I love Kirsty.'

'Well, it's just until I find someone else, then. I don't want to take advantage of you.' He reached out and tucked a strand of hair behind her ears in a distinctly brotherly gesture. 'Better put your hair back up or she'll tug it out by the handful.'

'Yes. That's probably a good idea. I'll put it up.' A ponytail was practical. Sensible. And that was the sort of person she was. Practical. She wasn't designed for grand passion or wild affairs. She was reliable, sensible Evanna. That was how other people saw her and it was how she should start seeing herself. No more dreams. No more fantasies.

He frowned down at her feet. *At her deliciously sexy, wickedly high-heeled shoes.* 'And you should probably wear something flat and comfortable. She can move like lightning now and you'll never be able to catch her in those. You'll twist your ankle.'

Something flat and comfortable. Something that reliable, sensible Evanna would wear. 'Right. I'll remember that, too.'

He reached out and squeezed her shoulder. 'You're a good friend, Evanna,' he said softly. 'The best.'

And then he turned and walked away from her, leaving her staring after him with all the hope lying shrivelled inside her.

She felt numb. Her limbs wouldn't move and for a moment she stood, staring through the curtain of green leaves, wondering what she was supposed to do now. She felt foolish in her dress and shoes and suddenly wished she'd just worn jeans.

That was it then.

Over.

It had been a foolish idea and it had failed.

And now she had to rejoin the group. Wearing her silly dress and her uncomfortable shoes, she had to talk and mingle and do all the things she usually did because if she didn't, everyone would notice. Everyone would know that something was the matter with her and she didn't want anyone to notice. *She didn't want people to know.*

Evanna blinked rapidly to clear the tears that had gathered and walked carefully on her new heels, brushing aside the fronds of the weeping willow, intending to help herself to some food. And then her eyes rested on Logan's broad, muscular shoulders and she found that she couldn't look away. Why did it have to be him? she wondered helplessly. Why him? Couldn't she have fallen in love with someone who noticed her? She stood there, drinking in his strength and masculinity, memorising every single part of him as if it were the last time she'd be allowed to look.

And then she felt Kyla's hand on her arm. 'Well? I saw him drag you into the weeping willow. The dress obviously worked.'

Evanna willed herself to move—*willed herself to act normally.* 'He wants me to look after Kirsty on Wednesdays. That's what he wanted to talk to me about.' Her voice sounded unnaturally formal, even to her own ears, and suddenly she knew she was going to cry. 'So I think we can safely say that the dress didn't impress him and that plan B has just crashed and burned alongside plan A. Will you excuse me? I'm suddenly incredibly tired. I think I'll go home and have an early night.'

'Evanna, you can't just—'

'I'll see you tomorrow, Kyla.' She needed to get away. Fast. Before she made a fool of herself.

Without looking back, she turned and walked quickly across the garden towards the gate. Let them say what they liked, she thought as she fumbled with the gate and walked to her car. She didn't care any more. She just needed to be on her own.

'Evanna, wait!'

Kyla's voice came from behind her but she ignored her and drove off without glancing back.

She drove the short distance to her cottage, parked the car and nearly twisted her ankle on the path that led to her front door. It was the final straw. With a sob of frustration she stooped and slid them from her feet, throwing them angrily on the grass. She struggled with her key, somehow managed to open the door of her cottage, even though her eyes were swimming with tears and she couldn't see clearly.

'Evanna.' Kyla was right behind her and she turned, all the emotions of the evening suddenly released.

'You didn't need to follow me. I didn't want you to. You're my best friend, Kyla, but there are some things that even best friends can't fix.' Her voice was choked. Clogged with tears. 'Leave me alone, please. I just need to be on my own for a bit.'

'But I can—'

'But you can what? *You can what, Kyla?* If you're even *thinking* about coming up with another plan to make your brother notice me, you can forget it because I already feel completely and *utterly* humiliated. He is never going to notice me, and the sooner I come to terms with that, the better for all of us.' She turned and sprinted up the rest of the stairs and into her bedroom.

'Evanna, wait, *please...*'

Evanna was holding back sobs, the breath tearing in her throat as she tried hard not to cry. 'Please, leave me alone. I need to be on my own.'

'No, you don't. You're upset and—'

'Can't you see?' Tears flooded down her face and Evanna gave up the struggle for control. 'Can't you see that this is *never* going to work? Aren't you satisfied? We changed the way I dressed and he simply thought I looked ridiculous! He told me to put my hair back up so that Kirsty wouldn't pull it and to wear something more flat and comfortable on my feet, and do you know what that is?' She ripped the dress from her body so violently that she tore the fabric. 'Because I'm not a flamenco dancer or anyone glamorous. I'm just me and it isn't enough.'

'Don't, Evanna.' Kyla reached out a hand to try and stop her but Evanna brushed her away, stepped out of the dress and reached for her comfortable dressing-gown.

'Enough!' The tears thickened her words as she quickly covered herself. 'You have to let it drop, Kyla, and so do I. When I was on the mainland I promised myself that this wasn't going to happen again. I wasn't going to keep hoping. No more jumping through hoops. No more waving flags that say, Here I am! No more humiliation. And now here I am yet again, crying over a man who doesn't want me. It has to stop. *It's got to stop.*'

Kyla's eyes were swimming with tears. 'I'm so sorry,' she whispered, and Evanna felt herself pulled into a warm hug. 'I'm so, so sorry.'

'Don't be sorry,' she said gruffly, wiping the tears from her cheeks with the flat of her hand. 'It's me who should be sorry for yelling at you. You're a good friend and you were only trying to help. It wasn't your fault. None of this is your fault. It's nobody's fault.'

'Yes, it is. It was me who forced you to dress up for him. I just know you'd be so amazing together.' Kyla's expression was stricken as she wiped the tears from her own face. 'I shouldn't have interfered, but I love both of you so much.'

Evanna reached for a tissue. 'And you can carry on doing that, but you have to love us separately. Logan and I are not a couple and we never will be. We can't be together.'

Kyla sank down on the edge of the bed. 'So what will you do now?'

'I'm going to do my job, help look after Kirsty and be a good friend to your brother.' Evanna blew her nose hard and kept her tone matter of fact. 'It's what he needs from me. It's what he wants.'

'But what about what you want?'

'What I want isn't important at the moment. What's important is Kirsty and Logan. He's been through hell and he needs support. And that's what friends are for.' Evanna looked up with a watery smile. 'You can have those shoes, if you like. I left them in the garden. You're the same size as me and I don't think I'll be wearing them again. Anyway, they pinched my toes.'

'Oh, Evanna…'

Evanna shook her head. 'I'm not a high heel sort of girl. I'm just me and—and he doesn't want me. And that's fine,' she said, blowing her nose for a final time. 'Deep down I always knew that I wasn't the right girl for him. I've just been deluding myself in the same way that all the other women on this island do. But he has no idea how I feel, so that's good. If he knew, that would make the whole situation incredibly embarrassing. As it is, we can carry on as if nothing has happened.'

She almost laughed as she listened to herself. Nothing *had* happened. Except in her dreams. And in her dreams was the only place that Logan was ever going to be.

CHAPTER FIVE

AFTER a sleepless night, Evanna woke with a pounding headache and gritty eyes to find Craig on the doorstep, ready to finalise the details for her bathroom.

'It's not even eight o'clock, Craig.' Her voice was croaky with lack of sleep and she dragged a hand through her tangled hair. 'And it's Sunday. Don't you have a home to go to?'

'I finished up at the Murray place last night so I thought I might as well come down here and get started as soon as possible. Can't get any peace at home, anyway, with our Molly waking everyone up at the crack of dawn.' He was wearing filthy overalls and Evanna led him through to the kitchen and put the kettle on.

'I can't string a sentence together until I've had a cup of coffee,' she muttered, spooning fresh coffee into a pot and adding the water. A delicious aroma filled the kitchen. 'What time does Molly wake up?'

'Five.'

Evanna winced. 'That's a wicked time to start the day.'

'She doesn't think so.' Craig rubbed his eyes with his fingers. 'We take it in turns to get up with her.'

'She's two. She ought to sleep later than that. Have you tried just leaving her?'

'Annie doesn't like to do that.' Craig gave a crooked smile. 'Can't bear her to cry. The moment she hears a murmur, she's in there.'

Evanna lifted two mugs out of the cupboard. 'It might be worth leaving her for a few minutes. She might just go back to sleep. Logan tried that with Kirsty a few months ago and it worked. She didn't even cry much, just whimpered a few times and then drifted off again.'

'Really? So you think that might work for Moll?'

'It's possible, but obviously you have to do what feels right for you. Here. Have some caffeine.' She handed him a brimming mug. 'I'm sure that we both need it.'

'Did I wake you? I assumed you'd be up.'

'I was up.' She hadn't really slept all night. She'd just stared at the ceiling, thinking about Logan, and now her eyes pricked angrily and her head ached. It was going to be a long day. 'Do you want to have another look at the bathroom?'

'That's what I was hoping.'

They walked upstairs and Craig wandered into her bathroom. 'I reckon it will take me and the lads about ten days,' he said, peering around the bathroom and scribbling something on a piece of paper. 'Providing there are no hitches.'

'My life is full of hitches,' Evanna said wearily, 'but we'll aim for the ten days. Will I be able to wash?'

'Yeah. Well, most of the time.' Craig frowned up at the ceiling. 'You want that painted the same blue as the rest?'

'Yes.'

'Nice. Looks like a seaside bathroom.' He nodded approval and then pulled out a tape measure. 'I'm going to cut some wood to fit there. Has all the stuff we ordered arrived?'

'It's blocking my garage as we speak.'

Craig stretched out the tape measure and recorded the length. 'That's a standard size. OK. We'll start tomorrow. I'll try and make sure the bath is only out of action for a few days. You can shower at Kyla's.' He tucked the pencil behind his ear and slid a finger over a pipe. 'We'll box this in for you. It will look better.'

'Whatever you say, Craig.' Evanna wished she could summon up more enthusiasm. 'As long as it looks like the picture I showed you, I don't care how you do it.'

'It's a shame we couldn't have fitted it in while you were on the mainland. Would have meant less disruption for you, but never mind.' He took a closer look at a hairline crack that was running across the ceiling. 'I bet Dr MacNeil is pleased to see you home. He told me Kirsty was missing you.'

Evanna tensed. 'She's growing fast.'

'No doubt about that.' He dropped to his haunches and studied the floor. 'This will have to come up. Those flashy Italian tiles you chose are going to look the business.'

'Thanks, Craig. I'll let you have a key so that you can just come and go while I'm at work.'

He stood up. 'There's going to be some dust and mess while we remove the old stuff, but I'll cover your carpet for you.'

Evanna waved him off and decided that, although it would be fun to have a new, luxurious bathroom, the process was obviously going to be unpleasant.

It wasn't even nine o'clock and suddenly the day stretched ahead of her. Before her trip to the mainland, she probably would have gone to Logan's and spent the day playing with Kirsty but now she was wondering whether that was the wrong thing for everyone.

While it was true that she was able to help with the little girl, it was also true that her constant presence was a disincentive to Logan to find someone else. And he needed to find someone else.

Remembering the look of sadness on his face the day she'd made lunch for them, Evanna resolved to try and think about someone who might suit him. Catherine had been wild and adventurous, so clearly that was the sort of woman who interested Logan and, offhand, she couldn't think of anyone who fitted that description.

Thinking about suitable partners for Logan did nothing for her piece of mind so she drank two cups of herbal tea, ate some fruit and wandered into her garden.

Although it was still early, the sun was already hot and it was obviously going to be another scorching day.

Deciding that the best cure for misery was a good exercise session before the weather became too hot to run, Evanna pulled on an old pair of shorts, slid her feet into her trainers and let herself out of the back door of the cottage.

The air was still, without a breath of wind, and the sea lay calm and quiet below the cliffs.

Forcing herself into a run, Evanna jogged steadily along the path, gradually increasing her pace.

She ran for almost half an hour, feeling the prickle of heat between her shoulder blades and the heat of the sun on her face. To her left the cliffs fell away steeply towards the sea and to her right were fields. Sheep grazed, placidly chewing on parched grass. Further inland was the rugged interior of the island, the province of walkers and climbers.

There had been no rain for weeks and the air smelt of sun and summer. The ground was hard under her trainers but still she ran, determined to chase away her gloom. It wasn't like her to be unhappy. She was, by nature, a happy, steady person. She wasn't given to fits of depression. So why did she feel so down?

Her pulse was thundering, her breath tearing in her lungs, and she pulled up for a brief rest, breathing heavily as she stared at the view. A few lone yachts bobbed on the water, barely moving in the still air. Apart from the occasional shriek of a seagull, it was completely peaceful. A lazy, quiet Sunday.

Later the tourists would crowd onto the beaches with their buckets and spades, but for now it was still too early for all but the most energetic of visitors to be up and about.

And then she glanced along the coast path and saw him.

Logan. And he had Kirsty on his shoulders.

Evanna let out a groan of frustration. Wasn't that just typical? Why did he have to be the one other person up and about? And how had she not realised that she'd run so far?

Kirsty waved her arms with excitement and Logan turned before she had time to vanish discreetly.

Wondering what terrible sins she'd committed to be forced to confront him in such a miserable, sweaty state, Evanna stood still, wishing she could wave a wand and transform herself. If she hadn't been feeling so dejected she would have laughed. Talk about going from one extreme to the other. Last night she'd worn a short dress and high heels and she'd been groomed to within an inch of her life. Today she was wearing her oldest shorts and a T-shirt with a half-faded slogan and her hair was a mess.

But what did it matter?

She'd never looked more feminine or glamorous than she had the night before, and had he noticed her? No. And if he hadn't noticed her in a dress and heels, why would he notice her in her ancient, practical running gear?

Logan just didn't find her attractive.

So she really didn't need to worry about him seeing her in her ancient shorts.

All the same she smoothed her damp hair away from her face as he approached. 'Hi. You're up early.'

'Kirsty hasn't learned to lie in yet. We make it until seven o'clock and that's good enough for me.' He reached up and lifted the toddler from his shoulders with strong hands. 'We thought we'd have an early walk to work up an appetite for a late breakfast.'

'Good idea.' *He looked good in shorts,* she thought. Logan had always been athletic and it showed in his physique. Dark hairs clustered at the open neck of his polo shirt and she looked away quickly, concentrating her attention on Kirsty, aware that he was looking at her.

'You hardly stayed for five minutes last night. Kyla said you weren't feeling that well.' There was concern in his voice. 'Are you sick? Bug of some sort?'

'No. No bug. I just felt a bit— I'm not sure—'

'You're not sure how you felt?'

Oh, for crying out loud, Evanna! 'I was just a bit tired.' She glanced out over the bay. 'It's going to be hot today.' Oh, help, she was reduced to talking about the weather.

'Yes.'

He was still looking at her. She could *feel* him looking at her and she turned to look up the coast path, afraid that he'd see something in her eyes that she didn't want him to see. 'I'm going to spend the afternoon cleaning out my bathroom, ready for Craig. He's starting tomorrow and—' She broke off and frowned slightly, squinting into the distance. 'What's the matter with them?'

Logan turned and looked. 'That couple? I walked past them about ten minutes ago. They're just tourists, out for an early stroll. They had a stack of newspapers in their rucksack. Probably looking for a peaceful spot on the headland to sit and catch up on the news. I can never understand that really, can you? People come to this island to escape from the big wide world and the first thing they do is buy a newspaper.'

'They're waving at us.'

'Why would they wave at us?' Logan lifted Kirsty off his shoulders and winced. 'She always holds onto my hair.'

'Logan.' Evanna caught his arm. 'They *are* waving at us. He's shouting something.'

Kirsty wriggled in Logan's arms and he shifted her back onto his shoulders in a smooth, confident movement. 'All right. Let's stroll back up there and see if there's something wrong.'

'There is something wrong. Definitely.' Evanna suddenly had a bad feeling. 'The woman's on the ground now. Has she collapsed or is she sitting down? I can't see properly from here.' She started to run along the path, aware that Logan was right behind her.

When she reached the couple the woman was on her knees and her hands were at her throat.

The man was right beside her. 'It's my wife, Alison. She's been bitten!' There was panic in his voice as he fumbled with his phone. 'I need to get help. I can't believe this has happened.'

'Bitten?' Evanna was already on her knees beside the woman. 'Bitten by what? Where?' She put a hand on the woman's shoulder in a gesture of reassurance and then closed her fingers around her wrist and felt her pulse. It was extremely rapid.

'It's a hundred and twenty, Logan.'

'Her foot. It's her foot. She trod on the damn thing. Oh, I can't do this.' The man's hands were shaking so much that he couldn't dial the number and the woman's breathing was becoming laboured.

She looked at her husband in blind panic and let out a sobbing breath. 'Pete—do something. My mouth's really dry and I feel dizzy. I didn't see it until I put my foot on it. *Do something.*'

Logan had transferred Kirsty from his shoulders to his arms but he didn't put her down because they were too close to the edge of the cliff. Instead, he held her easily and squatted down beside the woman, his voice calm and steady. 'Alison, try not to panic. I'm a doctor and I can help you but I need to know what happened. You said that something bit you? What was it? Insect?'

Alison turned her head to look at him and there was fear and revulsion in her eyes. 'Snake.' She croaked the word and Evanna frowned, thinking that she must have misheard.

'Snake? Are you sure?' Baffled, Evanna glanced around her but Logan didn't waste time questioning further. Instead, his fingers were on the woman's leg, examining an area that was reddening by the minute.

'Adder. It must have been an adder. Evanna, I want to bandage and splint the leg to stop her moving it around. What can we use?'

Still one step behind him, she stared at him blankly for a moment, tempted to answer, *Fresh air*. And then she saw something in his eyes—something serious—and his voice held an urgency that she didn't often hear. Logan was always calm and relaxed. It was unlike him to show that he was worried. 'I— You need a splint?' She thought quickly, her eyes flitting around her. 'Kirsty's cardigan? That's cotton so it would be fine as a pad. Your socks because they're longer and we can tie them, a folded newspaper as a splint?' Her improvisation clearly met with his approval because his blue eyes gleamed with approval.

'Let's do it.' Handing Kirsty to the woman's husband to hold, he dragged off his socks and thrust them into Evanna's hands. 'You'll be relieved to know that they've only been on my feet for about two minutes. You were reading the Sunday papers.' He turned to the woman's husband. 'Fold a section for me so that I have something rigid to use as support.'

The man dropped the phone, fumbled with the newspaper, cursing as he tried to fold it with hands made useless by nerves. Evanna reached over and took it from him, folded it neatly, placed it on the wound and they strapped the ankle.

Logan had the phone in his hand and was dialling. He made two calls—one to the air ambulance and one to Jim—and Evanna gave a swift nod of understanding. Jim owned the land they were walking on. The sheep in the field were his sheep and he owned a four-wheel-drive vehicle. Travelling cross-country, they could be in the surgery in less than five minutes.

Still holding Kirsty on one arm, Logan made the calls while Evanna glanced nervously around her. She'd lived on the island virtually all her life and she'd never seen a snake.

'What if it bites someone else? Should we look for it?'

'It will have gone. Adders are shy. They've been spotted on the island occasionally but they don't normally bother people. They feel the vibration of approaching walkers and slide away.'

'I think it must have been lying in the sun, warming itself,' the man muttered, dropping to his knees beside his wife. 'She trod on it and she was wearing sandals. It's summer. We didn't even bother with walking boots. We heard this terrific hiss and then she felt a really sharp stinging in her leg.'

'Can't breathe properly,' the woman gasped, lifting her hands to her throat, and Logan glanced across the fields.

'We're going to have you in the surgery in a couple of minutes,' he said easily, standing up and shielding his eyes from the sun. 'There's Jim now. I'm going to help you up, Alison, and we're going to get you into the car.'

Evanna looked at the woman's face, saw her increasing struggle for breath and wondered if they'd make it. Panic, with its sharp, deadly claws, stabbed through her and she looked at Logan, taking reassurance from the fact that he was so calm.

He was watching Alison and clearly working out a plan in his head. As Jim pulled up in his four-wheel-drive vehicle, Logan handed Kirsty to Evanna and lifted Alison inside. The rest of them clambered into the vehicle and Logan slammed the door shut.

'Drive,' he said to Jim, without wasting time on conversation or niceties and, to his credit, Jim rose to the challenge, covering the distance to the surgery in record time.

'I'll keep Kirsty with me,' Jim volunteered, and Logan gave a brief nod of thanks as he and Pete helped Alison out of the car.

Evanna unlocked the door and sprinted through to the consulting room. Without hesitating, she unlocked the drug cupboard and removed the adrenaline.

'Can you do a pulse and blood pressure, please? And let's give her some oxygen.'

Without hesitation, Logan helped Alison onto the couch, jabbed the injection straight into the muscle and depressed the plunger. 'Her pulse is a hundred and forty. I'm going to need more adrenaline, Evanna, and I want to do an ECG.'

'Her blood pressure is ninety over fifty.' Evanna quickly fastened a mask over the woman's mouth and nose and adjusted the flow of oxygen. Then she reached for the ECG machine and swiftly attached the leads.

'Ninety over fifty? That's low, isn't it? Is she going to be OK?' The woman's husband was pacing the floor, his hands clasping his head. 'I can't believe this has happened. I didn't even know that we had poisonous snakes in the UK. If I'd known, I wouldn't have let her walk in sandals. But it was hot and—'

'They rarely show themselves and the bite doesn't always cause such an extreme reaction. She was unlucky.' Logan took the second syringe from Evanna and injected the contents into his patient. 'Let's give her some antihistamine and hydrocortisone and I'm going to put a line in, just as a precaution.'

Evanna reached for the IV tray that she kept ready. 'Do you think she needs antivenin?' She knew nothing about antivenin but she knew that it existed.

'Possibly. She's obviously absorbed some venom.'

Evanna watched the ECG trace carefully but could see nothing amiss. 'That seems all right. What exactly are you looking for?'

'Non specific changes—ST depression or T-wave inversion.' Logan frowned and leaned closer. 'That seems all right. Leave it on until we transfer her to the helicopter. I want to keep an eye on it.'

'You're sending her to the mainland?' Evanna knew that

Logan never requested a helicopter transfer unless he was absolutely confident that the patient needed hospital help fast. In his years as the island GP, he'd shown himself to have an uncanny instinct for exactly when to call in the air ambulance.

'Yes.' His eyes were still on the ECG trace. 'Can you get the poisons unit on the phone for me? I want to talk to them.'

'Her blood pressure is coming up,' Evanna said, recording the reading and then reaching for the phone. She looked up the number and dialled swiftly, aware that Logan was examining his patient.

It was impossible to work with him and not admire him, she thought as she waited for someone on the other end to pick up the phone. In all the years that he'd been the doctor on Glenmore Island, she'd never seen him panic. *Even that awful night with Catherine, he'd been in control.* He was incredibly skilled and his confidence had a soothing effect on patients who were often anxious at finding themselves ill or injured so far from what they considered to be civilisation.

Logan removed the ad hoc dressing that they'd applied. 'Her leg is swelling up,' he said quietly, 'and I can see fang marks on her foot. So it was definitely a venomous bite. Do you know if her tetanus is up to date?'

'I have the poisons unit on the phone for you.' Evanna held out the phone and Logan stepped towards her and took the receiver.

'Can you clean and dress it, Evanna?' He lifted the phone to his ear. 'It's Logan MacNeil here.' His voice deep and steady, he swiftly outlined what had happened and discussed the best management with the person on the other end.

'Her colour looks better,' Pete said, and Evanna nodded as she checked her pulse again.

'Her breathing seems easier. We haven't even had a chance to take details from you. What's her surname?'

'Winchester. Alison Winchester. I'm Peter. We're staying at the Glenmore Arms. We only arrived yesterday.'

Evanna scribbled down the details and then checked the woman's pulse again and gave a nod. 'It's ninety-five now. Better. I'm just going to clean the wound and splint that leg properly.' She washed her hands, laid up a trolley and quickly cleaned and dressed the wound.

Logan replaced the phone. 'The air ambulance will be here any minute and we're going to transfer her to the mainland. They're expecting her in the hospital. I'll just write a quick letter so that they know what we've given.'

'I feel better.' Still pale, Alison lifted a hand to try and move the mask but Logan stopped her.

'Keep that on for the time being. The drugs I've given you are obviously taking effect and that's good, but we're going to fly you to the hospital on the mainland just in case you need some more treatment.'

'Will they keep me in?'

'It's likely, at least in the short term.'

'Are you going to go with her?' Evanna glanced out of the window as she heard the approaching helicopter.

'I ought to.' Logan's eyes were on the computer screen as he quickly drafted the referral letter. Then he pressed the print key and turned to look at her, and she read his mind.

Kirsty.

'I was just planning to have a quiet day so I'd be happy to have her,' she said softly, and he let out a long breath and ran his hand over the back of his neck.

'I feel guilty asking.'

'Don't. I love her, you know that. We'll have fun.' Evanna checked Alison's blood pressure again. 'That's much better. You go and talk to them, Logan.'

'Will I be able to go with her?' Pete glanced between the two of them and Logan nodded.

'That shouldn't be a problem. Unless you'd rather take your

car over on the ferry and drive. That way, you could pack a few things.'

'Yes, do that.' Alison shifted the mask slightly. 'I need you to bring me my night things and my bag from the bathroom. And I left my jewellery in the drawer by the bed. Better bring that, too.'

Evanna helped them transfer Alison to the helicopter and then went to check Kirsty.

'You might have warned me that she likes to pull hair. I've taught her to drive.' Jim grinned and Kirsty laughed with delight and held out her arms for a cuddle from Evanna.

'You and I are having a girls' day at home, Kirsty.' Evanna slid into the car. 'Jim, do you mind giving Pete a lift back to the Glenmore Arms? He's going to pack a few things, pick up the car and take the ferry to the mainland to be with his wife in hospital.'

'No problem. I'm due at work in half an hour anyway. Do you want to be dropped home?'

Evanna thought of all the preparation she'd planned to do on her bathroom and then dismissed it as unimportant. She could do it later. Her head ached and she didn't want to think about how tired she was. 'No, I'll spend the day here at Logan's. All Kirsty's toys are here. It will be easier to keep her occupied.'

It was mid-afternoon by the time Logan arrived home and Evanna and Kirsty were in the middle of an extremely messy painting session in the kitchen. She'd opened the sliding doors that led to the garden and a breeze cooled the stifling air.

'You put your hand flat, like that,' Evanna was saying as she planted Kirsty's hand in the middle of the paper and rocked it from side to side. 'Great!'

Logan stood in the doorway and watched. He loved the fact that Evanna wasn't bothered about the mess. She'd spread newspaper over the kitchen floor to protect it and then squeezed paint into saucers so that Kirsty could use her hands and feet, and Kirsty was bright-eyed with excitement. 'Whatever happened to reading a book or dressing a doll? I can't leave you two alone for a moment.'

Evanna glanced up, saw him there and scrambled to her feet, her cheeks flushed. She was still wearing the shorts and T-shirt that she'd been running in that morning, but she'd removed her trainers and her feet were bare. 'You know she loves painting. It's her favourite thing and I can't bring myself to say no. I've used plenty of newspaper so I'm hoping you won't be needing a new kitchen.'

'You spoil her,' Logan said softly, dropping his bag onto the nearest chair and removing his jacket. 'Amy used to hate doing anything messy because it meant clearing up, and she was always worried that Kirsty would splatter her with paint.'

'Well, I'm in my ancient running gear and I don't mind clearing up.' Evanna carefully lifted the paintings and put them outside on the table to dry in the sun, anchored by jam jars. 'How did it go with Alison?'

'I think they might give her antivenin. I've left her in their hands. She's in quite a bit of pain but her pulse and blood pressure have stabilised and her breathing has settled down. Hopefully she'll be all right now but they're going to keep her in for a bit just to check on her. Everyone is crowded around her, of course, because it's such an unusual thing to see.'

'I couldn't believe it was really a snake bite. I mean—' Kirsty was still planting her chubby little hands in the paint and Evanna stooped to adjust the newspaper on the floor '—we see a variety of accidents and illnesses on this island, but that was a first.'

'It's pretty rare.' Logan pulled open the fridge and removed a bottle of chilled water. 'And not often fatal in humans, although there are reports of severe allergic reactions and I thought Alison might have been one of those. Frustrating, actually, because you know I always carry adrenaline with me in the summer, ever since that wasp episode a few years ago. But Kirsty and I had only left the house for a quiet stroll so I didn't think of it. I had a nasty moment back there.'

'It didn't show. I think the fact that you were so incredibly calm helped to reassure Alison. Have you finished, sweetheart? That's a lovely painting. Clever girl.' Evanna lifted Kirsty, unconcerned about the volume of paint that was now attached to the child. 'I'm usually quite confident with emergencies, but not that one. I didn't want to speak in case I looked like a complete idiot. I had to stop myself from asking you stupid questions about first aid. I'm sure I read somewhere that you're meant to suck the venom out or something. Or cut the leg and let the blood flow.'

Logan drank the water straight from the bottle and then lowered his arm and smiled at her. 'You've been watching too much TV.'

'Actually, I never get to watch TV because I'm always working,' Evanna said with a pointed look. 'But there's so much myth and you hardly get copious amounts of experience in this country.'

She was so generous with Kirsty, Logan thought as he watched her. So patient. 'Well, these days more and more people keep dangerous snakes as pets and there's still some argument over best management and it does actually depend on the type of snake. But there is a body of medical evidence now and sucking and slashing isn't generally recommended.' Logan lifted the bottle and drank again. 'If you want to know about snake bites, Ethan is your man. He dealt with a few when he was working in Africa.'

Still holding Kirsty, Evanna glanced towards him. 'Really? I don't know how I feel about snakes. Sort of repelled and fascinated at the same time. I think if I'd met an adder on the path, I might have frozen with fright. I'm not surprised Alison felt a bit freaked out. Ugh.' She gave a shudder and Logan smiled, trying to imagine steady, practical Evanna freaking out about anything.

'It probably would have run away long before you saw it. To be honest, adders aren't generally a problem. They're shy.'

'But not this time.'

'She must have surprised it.'

'Well, she was lucky you were there.' Evanna wiped the worse of the paint from Kirsty's hands with kitchen roll and dropped it into the bin.

'I suppose so. I doubt the air ambulance would have made it quickly enough to deliver the adrenaline. That's why I decided that it was safer to take her to the surgery.' Logan threw the empty water bottle into the recycling bin. 'I'll talk to the warden about looking at the path. If they have a nest there, we should try and move it. We don't want a repeat of that, even though it was probably a one in a million chance. Is there anything to eat? I'm starving.'

'I made a chicken salad for your tea, but you could eat it now if you like.' Still with Kirsty on her hip, she walked to the fridge and pulled out a large white dish. 'I probably made too much but I thought you might be starving, having missed breakfast and lunch.'

'I am starving.' He looked at the dish and his mouth started to water. 'Is that your amazing chicken with the honey and lemon marinade?'

'That's the one.'

'My favourite. Have I ever told you that you're a genius in the kitchen, Evanna Duncan?'

A strange expression flickered across her face. 'Thank you.'

'Have you eaten?'

Evanna put Kirsty down on the floor. 'I should be going home. I still need to clear out my bathroom for Craig.'

Why was it, Logan mused, *that he always had the feeling she was trying to escape from him?* 'Share the salad with me.'

She hesitated and then gave a gasp of horror as she saw Kirsty crawling towards the white cupboards. 'No, angel. Not until I've washed your hands.' Smiling, she scooped the toddler into her arms and held her hands under running water, which turned blue and yellow as the splodges of paint faded and then disappeared. 'There. That's better. Now you're safe to have around. Just sit there a moment while I finish clearing up all the mess.'

She popped Kirsty on her bottom on the floor, carefully placed the paintings on the kitchen table to dry and swiftly gathered up the newspaper and disposed of it. Then she turned. 'Oh!'

Something in her voice made Logan look and he saw that Kirsty was up on her feet. While they both watched, she took a faltering step and then sank back onto her bottom with a satisfied grin.

'She walked!' Evanna clapped her hands with delight. 'Logan, she walked! You are a clever girl, Kirsty MacNeil. Let's see if she'll do it again.' She sank onto her knees and held out her hands. 'Walk to Evanna. Come on, Kirsty. Up you get!'

Kirsty scrambled to her feet again, swayed perilously and then took two steps before plopping back onto her bottom with a beaming smile.

'She's so pleased with herself!' Evanna grinned and scooped the child into her arms. 'Clever girl.'

'There'll be no peace for any of us now,' Logan predicted, captivated by the look of delight on Evanna's face. She was such a generous friend, he thought to himself as he picked up the salad and two plates. It was her day off and yet she'd willingly sacrificed it to look after his child.

And now she was eyeing the salad and the plates. 'I really ought to get home.'

'Not until you've eaten. Having given up your entire day for me, the least I can do is feed you, especially as you prepared the food.'

'You're the one who gave up your day, Logan,' she said quietly, opening a drawer and pulling out cutlery. 'I've been playing here with Kirsty. Hardly arduous. You've been working.'

'You have to join us, that's an order.' He winked at her and then watched, intrigued, as colour seeped into her cheeks. Why was she blushing?

'All right. You take the food out, I'll bring the drinks.'

They sat in the garden at the wooden table and Evanna held Kirsty on her lap and gave her breadsticks and chicken to eat. 'She's such a good eater. She loves my chicken.'

'We all love your chicken. That was the other thing about Amy.' Logan forked more salad onto his plate. 'She had a very limited repertoire in the kitchen. All she could cook was fish fingers.'

They ate in silence for a while and then Kirsty started to become fractious.

'She needs an early night,' Evanna murmured. 'I tried to put her down for a nap earlier but she was too wound up to sleep. She's tired.'

'You look tired, too.' Logan studied her face, noticing that her cheeks were paler than usual. 'Is something wrong? Did you have a bad night or something?'

'I'm fine.' She fussed around Kirsty and Logan suddenly had a strong suspicion that she was avoiding eye contact.

'Are you feeling ill? Because if you are then I can—'

'I'm not feeling ill, Logan. I'm fine. Really.' She stood up quickly, brushing a strand of hair out of her eyes and giving him a quick smile. 'If you're all right with Kirsty, I really ought to be going.'

He'd never known her so jumpy. 'Evanna.' He kept his voice

gentle. 'We're friends, aren't we? If there's something that you need to talk about, I hope you know that I'll always listen. You listen to my problems often enough. I hope you know that I'm here for you, too. This isn't a one-sided relationship.'

'I don't have a problem. There's nothing I want to talk about.' She handed him Kirsty and picked up her little rucksack. 'I'm going to make a move because I need to clear out the bathroom before Craig comes tomorrow.'

Why was she in such a hurry to leave? 'I'll give you a lift home.'

'You don't need to do that, I can walk. The exercise will be good for me. I was out for a run this morning when we met that couple so I didn't exactly finish my session.'

Was she ill?

Was she worried about something?

Seriously concerned, Logan would have pursued the topic but Kirsty was wriggling in his arms and he lifted her and decided to have a word with Kyla. She was Evanna's best friend. If something were wrong, Kyla would know. 'So you're happy to look after her on Wednesday afternoon?'

'Of course. It will be a relief to escape from all the mess and banging that will be going on at my house.' Evanna walked across the garden towards the gate. 'See you in surgery, Logan.'

She couldn't even behave normally around him any more, Evanna thought helplessly as she lengthened her stride and ran the distance back to her house.

All her life she'd felt more comfortable with Logan than any other person, but suddenly she felt awkward and uncomfortable in his company. It was becoming harder and harder to hide her feelings and obviously she wasn't succeeding any longer. He'd guessed that something was wrong. And that was typical of Logan, because he was extremely intuitive when it came to people.

Had he guessed how she felt about him?

No, of course he hadn't. Not yet.

But if she wasn't careful then he would, and then everything would change. She'd be mortified, he'd feel sorry for her—it would be completely hideous.

She shouldn't have stayed to eat with them. The moment he'd walked through the door she should have handed Kirsty to him and left. Playing house and getting cosy wasn't going to help her rehabilitation one bit. She'd never wean herself off Logan if she carried on spending this much time with him.

On Wednesday, things were going to be different, she promised herself as she let herself into her cottage. She'd stay with Kirsty until he arrived home and then she'd leave. No cosy chats. No supper in the garden.

Dropping her keys on the kitchen table, she went straight up to the bathroom for a shower.

She'd promised herself that she was going to build a life without Logan and that was what she was going to do.

CHAPTER SIX

'CAN you sign this prescription for me? I've changed Ann Carne's inhaler. I think she'd be better controlled on this.' Kyla stuck a prescription in front of her brother. 'I gather you had a busy Sunday.'

'Yes.' Logan signed with a flourish. 'Snake bite.'

'Good job Evanna was there to help.' Kyla took the prescription from him, her movements brisk and efficient. 'Would have been hard handling that on your own.'

'Yes. She was brilliant, as always. And then she took Kirsty for me while I went to the hospital.' Logan tucked his pen back in his pocket and looked at his sister. 'I wanted to ask you about her. Is she all right?'

'Why ask me? Why not ask her?'

'I did. I got the distinct impression that she was hiding something.'

'Like what?'

'I don't know.' Suddenly exasperated, Logan kept his eyes on his sister's face. 'Yesterday she looked pale. Tired. And she left the barbecue early. I just have a feeling that something is not right. She seems different. Jumpy.'

Kyla's gaze was direct. 'Well, you're the genius with women. I'm sure you'll figure out what's wrong.'

'That's why I'm asking you,' Logan said patiently. 'I thought you'd probably know. She's your best friend after all.'

'And best friends don't betray confidences.'

So there *was* something wrong. Logan sat back in his chair, genuinely concerned. 'If you know something, tell me. You have a duty to the practice to inform me of anything that affects my staff.'

'Your *staff?*' Kyla gave him a look of ill-disguised impatience. 'For goodness' sake, Logan, don't be so high and mighty! And try thinking about something other than work for five minutes, will you?'

He felt his shoulders tense. 'I'm not in the mood for a row, I just care about Evanna.'

'Do you?' Kyla looked at him, her gaze disturbingly direct. 'Really?'

Logan felt his own temper rise. 'Well, what sort of a question is that? Of course I care about her. Evanna has lived on this island all her life. She's a fantastic nurse and a really good friend. Frankly, I'm surprised you're not more worried about her yourself.'

'I'm worried,' Kyla said flatly. 'I'm very worried.'

'So you *do* know something.' Logan leaned forward, his voice a low growl. 'Tell me what's going on.'

'I dare say if Evanna has something she wants you to know, she'll tell you in good time. Thanks for the prescription.' Kyla walked towards the door and Logan stood up, his expression grim.

'Don't you dare say something like that and then leave the room.'

Kyla paused with her hand on the doorhandle. 'There's nothing I can tell you, Logan.'

The week flew by and by Wednesday afternoon Evanna was ready for a rest.

'I can't believe he's asked you to look after Kirsty,' Kyla grumbled as they exchanged notes after a busy clinic. 'What a nerve.'

'It isn't a nerve,' Evanna said calmly, dropping a soiled dressing into the correct bin. 'He needs someone that she's comfortable with. And, frankly, looking after Kirsty will be a pleasant change from looking after the rest of the population of this island. My feet are killing me and if I have to look at another case of sunburn I'm going to scream. It's the middle of August and it's blazing hot! Why don't people use sun block?'

'Because they're stupid,' Kyla said cheerfully. 'I've told Nick Hillier to arrest anyone who isn't wearing at least a factor twenty-five and lock them up until the sun goes down. And stop changing the subject. You're letting my brother take advantage of you.'

Evanna washed her hands and dried them. 'That's not true,' she said quietly, turning to face her friend. 'Logan and I have been friends for as long as you and I. He needs help and that's what friends are for. And anyway, if you saw the state of my house at the moment you'd understand why I'm only too happy to spend that afternoon at someone else's place.'

'You're too generous.'

'It isn't Logan's fault that I feel the way I do about him.'

'He asked me what was wrong with you.'

'Really?' Evanna stopped what she was doing. 'And what did you say?'

'Relax, I didn't tell him the truth, if that's what's worrying you, although I was very tempted. I told him that he should work it out himself. But obviously we're not going to hold our breath on that one because you've been in love with him for twenty-six years and he hasn't worked it out yet.' Kyla suppressed a yawn and made for the door. 'I'm still thinking about plan C.'

'What's plan C?'

'Hitting him over the head with an extremely hard object. I thought it might bring him to his senses.'

Evanna managed a smile. 'I'm relieved he doesn't know. Can you imagine how awkward it would be if he found out how I felt?' She gave a shudder and Kyla looked at her thoughtfully.

'Maybe it would just be a relief.'

'I don't think public rejection could ever be a relief,' Evanna said flatly. 'It's bad enough loving him, without him knowing. At least spare me that.'

'But if he knew, maybe he'd—'

'Don't.' Evanna interrupted her with a lift of her hand. 'Just don't even go there! You can't change a man's feelings. I'll see you tomorrow.'

She let herself through the door that connected with Logan's house and relieved Meg, who had been looking after Kirsty all morning.

The weather was stifling and Kirsty hot and short tempered and they spent the afternoon playing and reading books under the shade of the weeping willow.

Once Logan arrived home, Evanna made for the door, ruthlessly squashing the temptation to linger and chat. *And be with him.*

'Craig is tearing my bathroom to pieces so I need to go and scowl at him just to be sure he doesn't get too carried away. Looking at the mess at the moment, I can't believe it's ever going to look even half-decent.'

She arrived home to find her cottage in chaos. The front door was open and half her old bathroom was lying in the front garden.

'Remind me never to contemplate having anything more adventurous than the bathroom done.' She picked her way through a pile of dust and rubble. 'Craig, tell me that this is going to look good when you've finished. Please, tell me that.'

He pushed his hair out of his eyes with a grubby hand and

grinned. 'It's going to be stunning. The taps arrived today. They're great. You've got good taste, Nurse Duncan.'

Evanna sighed and tried not to look at the mess. 'So how long am I going to be without a bath?'

'A few days. I hear the helicopter was out twice on Sunday.'

'Yes.' Evanna tried not to look at the mess. 'Typical August, really.'

'And you've been helping Dr MacNeil with the little one.' Craig rubbed his forehead with the back of his hand. 'The man needs a wife. I dare say he'll meet someone else soon enough.'

Was it her imagination or was he giving her a funny look? 'Very possibly, but in the meantime he's managing perfectly well on his own.' Evanna remembered what Logan had said about everyone telling him he'd meet someone else. 'He's doing fine.'

'Still—nice of you to help him.'

'I've known Logan since I was born,' Evanna said evenly. 'He's one of my closest friends.'

'Of course he is. And you and Kyla have been thick as thieves since you were both in nappies.' Craig stared out across her garden. 'Sometimes you don't notice something when it's been in your face all your life.'

Was it that obvious to everyone? 'Craig—'

'He's single. You're single. Seems perfect to me.'

Evanna stared at him with a mixture of exasperation and embarrassment. Was everyone thinking the same as Craig? 'Anna Brice is single, too, Craig,' she said in a tart voice. 'Why not just pair her up with him.'

'Possibly because she's eighty-six on her next birthday.' Craig scratched his arm. 'It isn't just because you're both single that I think you'd be good together. You're friends. Everyone can see that.'

'Marriage is about far more than just friendship,' Evanna said briskly, and Craig gave a nod.

'Perhaps. But it's a good start.'

Evanna thought of the passion that Kyla and Ethan shared. She thought of the looks they exchanged and the way that they touched all the time. It was as if they couldn't be near each other and not be joined.

She wouldn't settle for less.

'I need to get on, Craig.'

'Of course you do, what with a busy morning in the surgery and a busy afternoon at Dr MacNeil's. I'll just finish up here and get out of your way.' He beamed at her. 'Is seven too early to start tomorrow? I like to get the heavy stuff done before the sun comes up.'

'Seven is fine. Thanks, Craig.'

One of the problems of living in a small community, Evanna reflected as she stepped over the rubble and walked into her kitchen, was that everyone was far too interested in everyone else.

She just hoped that no one said the same thing to Logan.

The next week passed in a blur as the surgery handled an unprecedented number of tourists.

'I feel as though I'm running an A and E department,' Logan grumbled as he and Evanna cleared up after stitching yet another child who had slipped on the rocks. 'That was a nasty cut.'

'He was rock-pooling and he should have been wearing shoes and not flip-flops. I suppose he just didn't have any grip, which was why he slipped.' Evanna dropped the stitch cutter into the sharps box. She'd been making a supreme effort to behave naturally with Logan and it seemed to be working. At least he'd stopped asking her if anything was wrong.

'People leave their brains behind when they're on holiday. I heard from the hospital today about Alison Winchester. They kept her in for a night and then followed her up before she went back down to London. She was still suffering aches and pains but no other effects that they can see. They've written to her GP.'

'That will be a first for him. I bet a GP in London would know even less about an adder bite than I did.' Evanna walked across the room and washed her hands. 'Did they manage to find the snake, by the way?'

'Funnily enough, yes. The park ranger rang me last week. They've relocated the family.'

'Mr and Mrs Adder.' Evanna laughed, yanking paper towels out of the holder. 'Somewhere homely with a nice view, I hope. Hot and cold running water.'

'Somewhere that no one is going to tread on them again, I hope,' Logan said dryly, sitting down and hitting a key on the computer. 'Am I finished here?'

'For now. Janet told me that you have three house calls. Doug is feeling really dizzy and wondered if you'd call on your way home. I suspect it's the heat or maybe his tablets, but it's worth checking. You know how worried he's been since they discharged him from the hospital.'

'Patients are always worried after a heart attack and it's still relatively early days for Doug.' Logan picked up a set of results and scanned them. 'How's Sonia's blood pressure at the moment?'

'It's still on the high side but her urine is fine and she has no swelling.'

Logan pulled a face and leaned back in his chair. 'I still feel uneasy about her, Evanna. I'd rather she was in hospital.'

Evanna felt a twist of sympathy. 'It's natural that you'd worry after what happened with Catherine, but so far there isn't an indication to admit her. I'm calling on her every day and if there's any change, we'll transfer her to the mainland in plenty of time.' Her eyes met his and she knew what he was thinking. That night, the horrible storm, losing Catherine because the helicopter hadn't been able to reach the island.

'Logan...' She hesitated, unsure whether to speak or not. 'You know that there was nothing else you could have done, don't you?'

'Yes.' His voice was harsh. 'But knowing that doesn't make it any easier to live with.'

'I know that. I was there, too.' Evanna swallowed, remembering the night with a shudder of cold panic. 'And I ask myself every day whether I could have done something different. Whether I should have spotted something.'

He ran a hand over his face and let out a long breath. 'There was nothing, we both know that. Catherine had an undiagnosed cardiac problem. Even if she'd been in hospital, the outcome would have been the same.'

'You were amazing, Logan.' She bit her lip, desperately wanting to comfort but not knowing how. 'You saved Kirsty and look how bonny she is.'

'Yes.'

Evanna hesitated. 'You should go out more, Logan. I'll babysit for you so that you can have dinner or something.'

He lifted an eyebrow, a flicker of humour in his blue eyes. 'With whom, exactly?'

'I don't know.' Evanna blushed, wishing that she'd never brought the subject up. It was bad enough thinking of Logan with another woman, without actually putting a face and name to someone. 'I just think you need to get out. Have a social life.'

He frowned. 'I have a social life. I see Kyla and Ethan. Meg and the cousins. You. We're always eating together and spending time on the beach.'

Her heart skipped. 'I know that. I was talking about... romance.'

'I'm not interested in romance.' His gaze was steady. 'Maybe I will be one day, but not at the moment.'

'Then that's fine. I'm not pushing you. I'm just saying that whenever you're ready, I'll help. I just want you to know that I'll babysit.' She decided that it was time to change the subject. 'You've been great with Lucy. She tells me that she's always ringing you in a panic about something and that you're incredibly patient.'

'She's a new mother. It's natural to worry. I keep meaning to pop in and see her but Ethan and I have just been too busy.' His eyes lingered on her face for a moment. 'How's she getting on?'

'Fine.' Evanna nodded. 'Sweet, actually. She's so in love with that baby.'

'Lucy is a nice girl. No problems, then?'

'No. The feeding is going well, the baby is starting to sleep a bit longer and I've seen Lucy out and about, pushing her in the pram, several times this week.'

'Good.' Logan glanced at his watch and stood up. 'Right, then. I'll get on with my house calls. It's Wednesday.' He frowned as if he'd only just realised that fact. 'Are you all right to look after Kirsty again this afternoon?'

'Of course. It's what we agreed. I hadn't forgotten. Believe me, it's a relief to escape from the banging and the blaring radio in my house. Why do builders always need the radio on full blast? I've eaten my way through two packets of paracetamol since they started and I'm sick of making bacon sandwiches for hungry men.'

Logan picked up his bag. 'You spoil people, that's your problem. Most builders are lucky to be given a dry biscuit.'

'I suppose I always feel that they'll do a better job if I've fed them properly,' Evanna said gloomily. 'I still can't quite believe that this bathroom is going to look nice when it's finished. There's dust everywhere and the walls are full of holes.'

'Craig is a reliable guy. And if he messes up your bathroom, I won't sign his repeat prescriptions.' Logan walked towards the door and then turned. 'By the way, the cleaner cancelled this morning so my house is going to be a complete mess, but just ignore it. Hopefully she'll be able to make it tomorrow. Anyway, by the time Kirsty has finished throwing her toys around, you'd never know a cleaner had been near the place. It always strikes me as a complete waste of money.'

'Spoken like a true man. I've bought a couple of new books for her. I thought I'd take her down to the beach for a picnic tea once it gets a bit cooler.'

'Good idea. If I finish my surgery early enough, I might join you down there.' He glanced at his watch. 'I'd better dash. Thanks, Evanna.'

'You're welcome.'

She watched him go and then lifted a hand to her ponytail. It was a good job he didn't notice her as a woman, she thought wryly, glancing at her reflection in the mirror. She hadn't been able to wash her hair for two days because Craig had turned the water off and now there was some problem with the plumbing that wasn't likely to be fixed for at least another day.

She was desperate for a shower or a bath but Kyla had a houseful of guests so she hadn't liked to ask.

And then a thought occurred to her.

What was stopping her having a shower at Logan's? She had a change of clothes in her bag ready for the afternoon, and Kirsty would be perfectly happy to play in the bathroom for five minutes while she washed her hair and scrubbed off all the dust and dirt that seemed to have stuck itself to her during the bathroom renovation.

She walked through the door that connected the surgery to Logan's house and smiled at Meg. 'My shift.'

'I don't know how you manage her,' Meg said wearily, handing over a wriggling Kirsty. 'All I do is spend the morning pulling her away from danger. I had all sorts of plans for cleaning and ironing and I've done nothing except wrestle with her. And as for feeding her—I'd swear that girl doesn't know where her mouth is. I had to change her twice during breakfast. There was porridge on the walls and the ceilings.'

'Have you been a handful?' Evanna kissed Kirsty's cheek and popped her down on the floor. 'Don't worry about the house, Meg. She'll probably have a nap in a minute. I'll try and catch up on a few things while she sleeps.'

'Don't you go doing Logan's cleaning.' Meg frowned her disapproval as she gathered her things together. 'It's good of you to look after Kirsty, without sorting out his mess.'

'I'm happy to help, Meg,' Evanna said softly, smiling at Kirsty who giggled and clapped her hands. 'I know it isn't very fashionable to admit it, but I love cleaning and keeping house.' Only she didn't have anyone to do it for, except herself.

'Well, if Kirsty lets you so much as lift a teatowel, it will be a miracle. I need to dash because apparently the café is heaving with tourists.' Meg leaned towards Kirsty and waved a finger. 'Now, you be a good girl!'

Kirsty beamed and waved. 'Byee-ee.'

'Oh!' Evanna gasped with delight. 'I didn't know she'd learned that!'

'Now, don't you go being soppy about her—she's a cheeky monkey. And she knows exactly how to get round you.' Meg slipped her bag onto her shoulder and made for the door. 'Have a good afternoon. Pop in for an ice cream if you feel like it. I'll make her one of my specials.'

Evanna waited for the door to close behind her and then settled down on the floor next to Kirsty, who was rubbing her eyes. 'You've had a busy morning. Are you tired, pickle? Where's your blanket?' She looked around for the little pink blanket that Kirsty always slept with and spotted it lying over the back of a chair. 'Let's take you up to bed and see if you feel like a nap.'

She changed Kirsty's nappy, gave her a drink of milk and then settled her in the cot with her blanket. Immediately Kirsty's eyes drifted shut.

'Creating trouble for Meg obviously wore you out,' Evanna murmured with amusement, creeping out of the room and leaving the door open a crack.

She glanced longingly at the bathroom but then decided she may as well tidy the house before she finally had the wash she'd been fantasising about for hours.

For the next hour she worked like a demon. She neatly stacked all Logan's medical journals, she scooped clothes from the floor and put them in the washing machine, she tidied and scrubbed the kitchen until all the surfaces were gleaming, she mopped the floor, ran the dishwasher and emptied all the bins.

Then she threw open all the doors and windows to air the place. Logan's house was lovely, she reflected as she plumped the cushions on his soft, comfortable sofa. So airy and light. It was a little further from the beach than hers, but she loved the space and all the windows and she adored his garden. As well as the weeping willow there were four huge apple trees that provided plenty of dappled shade. A large white hammock was strung between two of the trees and a children's book and several toys were lying abandoned on the grass. Logan had obviously been out there with Kirsty. Evanna looked at the hammock longingly. *Later,* she promised herself. Maybe she and Kirsty would curl up in the hammock to read books.

She chopped vegetables ready to add to the casserole that she planned to make later and then looked at the clock. Kirsty had been asleep for an hour and a half.

Feeling horribly hot and sticky after her efforts on the house, Evanna dragged her forearm over her forehead and decided to check on the child.

She crept upstairs and peeped around the door but the little girl was still fast asleep, the tip of her thumb in her mouth.

Evanna closed the door again and decided that she just about had time for a quick shower before the toddler woke up. Then she'd make the casserole for supper. She could give it to Kirsty for tea and Logan would be able to eat the remains when he finished work.

She walked into the bathroom that she'd cleaned earlier. Oh, the bliss of not having to pick her way through rubble! Swiftly she stripped off her clothes and stepped under Logan's state-of-the-art power shower. Five minutes. That was all it would take. And, by then, Kirsty should be ready to wake up.

Logan opened the front door and walked into his house. Bracing himself for the usual noise and activity, he was surprised to find the house silent. Then he remembered Evanna mentioning that she might take Kirsty to the beach.

The morning post was neatly stacked on the hall table and he could see at a glance that both the kitchen and the living room were immaculate. Meg had already called him to apologise for the fact that she hadn't managed to touch any of the housework, thanks to the demands of his daughter, so he knew that only one person could be responsible for the sudden transformation of his house.

Evanna.

She must have cleaned for him. She was a born nurturer, he thought as he noticed the polished kitchen floor and the vegetables chopped ready for a casserole. Always caring for people whether she was on or off duty. Feeling a twist of guilt, he ignored the post and walked upstairs towards his bedroom. He'd just find the textbook he needed, make himself a cup of tea and then get back to the surgery and tackle the mountain of paperwork that awaited him.

As he reached the top of the stairs, the bathroom door opened and Evanna walked out.

Naked.

And dripping wet.

Logan stared and then he almost swallowed his tongue.

Her legs were long and slender, her hips wonderfully curved and her breasts full and crowned by rosy pink nipples which glistened with drops of water from the shower.

'Evanna!' He croaked out her name and she froze to the spot and her eyes widened and locked with his.

For a long, pulsing moment they both stood. Staring.

The atmosphere crackled with tension and then she came to her senses, gave a squeak of horror and looked around desperately for something to cover herself up with, but there was nothing. 'I forgot to grab a towel—I—I was— You can't look—*Logan!*' Her voice was tortured with embarrassment as she glared at him. '*Stop* looking at me! It's not very gentlemanly.'

Gentlemanly?

At any other time Logan would have laughed at her use of such an old-fashioned word but he was too busy being thoroughly ungentlemanly to respond. In fact, he didn't really know what he was doing. His brain had ceased coherent thought and his eyes were definitely under independent rule. It wasn't until she moved her hands down to cover herself that he realised his gaze had been firmly fixed on the tempting shadows between her legs.

All the oxygen seemed to have been sucked out of the air and Logan suddenly couldn't breathe properly.

She was still trying to shield herself with her hands but he already had an all too clear image of her lush feminine curves imprinted on his brain.

He'd known Evanna for his whole life and he'd thought that he knew everything there was to know about her. He knew that she was kind, endlessly patient and had a good sense of humour.

He knew how she liked her coffee, he knew that she liked to run and swim. He knew that at school she'd been top in English but hopeless at maths. She was his sister's best friend and he knew her well. Really, really well. Up until today he would have said that there was nothing about Evanna that he didn't know.

So why hadn't he known that she had a body straight out of a hot male fantasy?

Gripped by lust, he closed his eyes briefly to try and erase the image and dragged a towel from the cupboard.

'Here…' His voice hoarse, he clutched the towel, intending to hand it to her and move away, but he couldn't prevent himself from taking one more look and then found he couldn't stop looking. The creamy skin of her shoulder and the tempting swell of her breasts were more addictive than any drug.

She had fantastic breasts.

Had she always had those breasts or had she suddenly grown them?

Why had he never noticed her breasts before?

Jabbing his fingers through his hair, he tried to look away but his eyes just wouldn't obey his brain. Her hair was soaking wet and hung halfway down her back, and she was deliciously slippery and gleaming wet after her shower. His mouth dried and he realised that any moment now he was going to power her back against the wall and take her. Hard. 'I— You—'

'For crying out loud, Logan, *stop staring!*' Her voice sounded strangled and her expression was horrified as she snatched the towel and held it in front of her. 'You've seen me in a bikini a million times so I don't see why seeing me naked is such a big step.'

Had he seen her in a bikini? His mind dulled by lust, Logan struggled to think. Yes. He *had* seen her in a bikini. So why hadn't he ever noticed her body before? Was he blind? Stupid? *Both?* Lost in an explicit fantasy involving his hands and mouth on those delicious curves, it took him a minute to realise that she'd asked him a question. 'What? Sorry?'

She stared at him in exasperation. 'What is the *matter* with you? I asked you what on earth you were doing here, anyway.'

Taking a fast ride to paradise? 'I live here. I think.' He wasn't sure of anything any more.

'Well, I know that you live here. I'm not stupid.' She tightened her grip on the towel, trying to hold it in place. 'But I wasn't expecting you home. You're *supposed* to be working.'

He'd never heard Evanna snappy before but she was decidedly snappy and he found her efforts to maintain her dignity and privacy incredibly endearing. Water clung to her dark lashes and her cheeks were pink with embarrassment.

'I was working,' he drawled softly, 'but I wanted—I needed…' He couldn't remember what he wanted or needed because it had been superseded by something else entirely. *Her.*

'Oh, forget it! It doesn't matter now.' She interrupted him and backed into the bathroom, glaring at him as if he'd committed a terrible sin.

And he hadn't. Not yet.

But in another moment he might do just that.

The temptation to just grab her and bring his mouth down on her soft, pink lips was so overwhelming that he clenched his fists by his sides, just to make sure that he wasn't tempted.

'Oh, this has got to be the most embarrassing moment of my life,' Evanna muttered, pushing the door closed between them and leaving it open just a crack. 'Stop staring and pass me my clothes.'

'Clothes?'

'Yes, Logan,' she snapped. '*My clothes!* They're in a pile on the floor outside the bathroom door. Get a grip! Did you leave your brain behind at work?'

In all the years he'd known her, he'd never heard Evanna irritable before. She was the most tolerant, patient person he'd ever met but suddenly she was behaving as though he'd done something grievously wrong.

'Evanna.' He tried to keep his tone mild. *Tried to sound indifferent.* 'There's no need to be embarrassed. I've known you all my life.'

And he'd obviously been walking around with his eyes shut!

'Well, that doesn't mean I want to stand in front of you stark naked! My clothes, Logan! They're in the bag by your feet. And don't you *dare* ever breathe a word of this to anyone. If I am on the receiving end of a single knowing wink when I walk into the pub, you'll be finding yourself a new practice nurse.'

Logan dutifully found the bag and handed it to her. She virtually dragged it from his hand and closed the bathroom door firmly in his face.

Logan stared at the wood. He could have told her that it didn't make any difference, hiding behind a door or a towel. He could have told her that the image of her lush, naked body was now firmly fixed on his *extremely* over-heated brain. But he thought that in her current mood she just might hit him so he stayed silent and tensed slightly when she dragged open the door and faced him.

She was wearing skimpy shorts and an ancient T-shirt in a washed-out, faded blue and her long, damp hair was caught up in a ponytail.

She looked like the old Evanna. Except that she didn't. Because now he knew.

He knew what was underneath the clothes.

'I'm dressed,' she said through gritted teeth, thrusting the damp towel into his hands, 'so you can stop standing there, gawping.'

'Evanna—'

'Oh, grow up!' Her cheeks flushed a deep shade of pink and she scurried into Kirsty's room, leaving Logan staring after her.

Aware that he needed to pull himself together, he drew in a deep breath and tried to think about something boring and inconsequential. Anything that would take his mind off the vivid image of Evanna's naked body. Since Catherine's death he hadn't thought about a woman—*hadn't wanted a woman.*

Until now.

Frustrated and taken aback by the strength of his own reaction, he suddenly knew that he had to get out of the house before he did something that would embarrass both of them. This was Evanna. They were friends, for goodness' sake. Somehow he had to erase that image from his mind and go back to the way he'd seen her previously—as a colleague and a lifelong friend. *The best friend he had.* Thoughts of sex had never intruded on their relationship before and he couldn't let it now.

If she knew just how much she'd affected him, she'd feel awkward. Their entire relationship would change. They wouldn't be able to work together properly. They...

Swearing softly, he retreated back downstairs, pushed open the door that connected his house to the surgery and walked back to his consulting room without any hope of being able to concentrate.

Evanna held her head in her hands and tried not to scream.

How could she have been so *stupid?*

Wasn't it perfectly obvious that he'd come home the minute she'd chosen to take a shower in his bathroom? Wasn't life always like that?

Tortured by embarrassment, Evanna resisted the temptation to hide under Kirsty's cot and never come out again.

The little girl was wide awake, lying on her back, hugging her blanket and sucking her thumb, oblivious to the turmoil that Evanna was suffering.

Why hadn't she at least remembered to take a towel into the bathroom with her?

What had possessed her to walk out of the bathroom, naked?

And why hadn't he just done the gentlemanly thing and looked away? Why hadn't he given her one of his cheeky smiles and covered his eyes?

It didn't even help to tell herself that he'd seen her in a swimming costume a million times because never, when he'd seen her on the beach, had he ever reacted with such stunned amazement.

Did she really look that awful?

Anyone would think he'd never seen a naked woman before, she thought crossly, lifting Kirsty from her cot and giving her a hug. Which was nonsense, because everyone knew that Logan Alastair MacNeil had had a fearsome reputation with women until he'd met and married Catherine. There were some on the island who'd thought he'd never settle down. So, for him to stand there with his mouth open as if he were shocked to see a naked woman was ridiculous, because she happened to know that he'd seen more than his fair share of naked women in his time.

'Oh, Kirsty, I've never been so embarrassed,' she whispered, delaying the moment until she had to leave the safety of the bedroom. But Kirsty was full of energy after her sleep and dying to play so she had no choice but to take her downstairs.

Determined to behave as though nothing had happened, Evanna lifted her chin and carried the toddler into the kitchen.

But there was no sign of Logan.

Unnaturally jumpy, Evanna looked around, called his name and then peeped out of the front door, but there was no sign of his car.

He'd gone.

Without even saying goodbye.

'Nice to know that seeing me naked had such an amazing effect on him,' Evanna grumbled as she pulled a fromage frais out of the fridge for Kirsty. 'Did he grab me and kiss me senseless? No. Was he so overwhelmed by the sight of my wet, naked body that he couldn't keep his hands off me? No. What does he do? He just stares, stammers like an idiot and then walks off without even bothering to say goodbye. I tell you, Kirsty MacNeil, you should have been born a man. It's a lot easier than being a woman, believe me.'

CHAPTER SEVEN

'SONIA'S blood pressure is still high. She's made an appointment to go to the hospital on Monday for a check.' Evanna put some forms on the desk in front of Logan, not meeting his eyes. But he was watching her.

She could feel him watching her.

'Good. I don't mind admitting that I'd be far happier if they kept her in.'

It was two days after what Evanna now called 'the bathroom incident', and every time they came into contact with each other, they skirted round the issue, each of them incredibly formal with the other, and Evanna was starting to despair that she'd ever be able to behave naturally again.

And he wasn't behaving naturally either.

It would have helped if he'd laughed or made some sort of light-hearted comment, but he hadn't referred to it. Not only that, but he hardly looked at her when she walked into the room.

It was enough to make a girl lose every scrap of confidence. 'Janet wanted to know if you'd like some more coffee.'

'Yes, please.' His voice was terse. 'I need the caffeine to keep me awake. I had a terrible night. Again.'

Evanna hesitated. Two days ago, *before the bathroom incident,* she would have been concerned enough about that statement to question him further, but now she didn't dare because she was suddenly horribly aware of everything about him and the effect he had on her was incredibly frustrating.

She just didn't know what to say or do. And clearly he felt the same way because he made no effort to detain her when she scurried towards the door.

'I'll ask Janet to bring you some coffee.' She delivered the message to the kindly receptionist and retreated to the safety of her own room, finished her clinic and then restocked and tidied until she could be sure that Logan would have left on his house calls.

'Logan's looking terrible,' Janet clucked as she locked the surgery door. 'Four cups of coffee he's asked for this morning. It's a wonder his hands aren't shaking too much to hold his stethoscope. And the same yesterday.'

'Kirsty's probably keeping him awake,' Evanna mumbled, as she returned a set of notes she'd borrowed. 'Disturbed nights.'

'Well, you can tell from the shadows under his eyes that he's having disturbed nights, but I don't think Kirsty is the culprit.' Janet checked the clinic list for the afternoon. 'He told me only yesterday that she goes right through the night now, bless her.'

'So what's keeping him awake?' Evanna delved into her bag for her keys and Janet gave a sigh.

'I don't know, but I was hoping you did. You're the one he talks to, Evanna. Through all of last year when he was struggling to keep everything going, you were the only one he really talked to.'

Evanna stilled. It was true. Logan had found her easy to talk to. But since she'd stripped naked in his bathroom, he'd hardly spoken a word to her that didn't revolve around patient care.

Which meant only one thing. Clearly he felt as awkward about the whole incident as she did, which was entirely ridiculous, she told herself as she waved goodbye to Janet and made for the door. They'd known each other all their lives. Surely they could get themselves past one embarrassing incident?

If he wasn't going to tackle the subject then she would. She'd mention it and dismiss it as if the whole incident had been nothing more than a laugh.

Logan kept the top down on his sports car, hoping that the breeze might clear his head.

Four cups of coffee and a splash of cold water on the face had done little to revive him and he vowed to have an early night.

Then he remembered that an early night was going to make no difference whatsoever. It wasn't going to bed that was a problem, it was sleeping when he got there. Eyes open or eyes shut, he saw Evanna. Naked. Her creamy, smooth skin still glistening and damp from the shower, her hair trailing down her back. It had been two days since he'd walked in on her but he couldn't erase the image from his brain.

He felt himself grow hard and cursed repeatedly, jabbing the car into gear more viciously than was necessary.

He was afraid to stand up when she walked into a room in case she noticed the effect she had on him.

What was the matter with him?

Why was his reaction so extreme?

Was it just because he hadn't had sex since Catherine's death? And so what if it was? What could he do about it? He was hardly likely to go up to Evanna and suggest that they spent a steamy night between the sheets together, was he? What was he supposed to say? *Oh, good morning, Nurse Duncan. Doug McDonald's blood pressure has come right down on his new drug regime and, by the way, do you fancy stripping naked and sleeping with me because I can't get your body out of my head?*

Suffering from an intense bout of male frustration, Logan pulled the car to the side of the road and switched off the engine.

He sat for a long moment just staring out across the sparkling sea while he sifted through the options.

Forget the whole thing, that was the obvious option. But he'd just spent an extremely frustrating two days trying to do exactly that, and it hadn't worked. So forgetting her wasn't an option.

But what was the alternative?

Tell her how he felt? Ask her out?

He almost laughed as he anticipated her reaction. He'd known Evanna all her life. If he asked her out, she'd laugh and, anyway, they already spent a great deal of time together. She was in and out of his house, helping him with Kirsty and joining his extended family for meals. She was his sister's best friend. How was he supposed to make it clear that he wanted the time they spent together to be different? How was he supposed to let her know that when he asked her to spend time with him, it wasn't a platonic invitation.

How did you turn a deep and lasting friendship into a love affair?

The answer was that you didn't.

If anything were going to happen between them, it would have happened years ago. When they'd been teenagers, fooling around on the beach. When she'd had sleepovers with Kyla. When they'd started working together. They'd had so much opportunity.

And if Evanna had felt anything for him at all, why would she have been so appalled that he'd seen her naked?

There was no way she could have failed to be aware of his reaction to her.

And yet she hadn't flirted or even laughed. She'd been shocked. Embarrassed. Unable to hide herself quickly enough.

Hardly the reaction of a woman keen to alter the status of their relationship.

If he showed her how he felt and she rejected him, it would make their working situation intolerable.

Which meant that somehow he had to get his feelings under control.

Somehow he had to behave as if nothing had happened.

As if he wasn't constantly fantasising about her body.

It was impossible to miss the irony of the situation, he thought to himself as he ran a hand over his face and breathed out heavily. *Finally,* he was interested in a woman again. For the first time since Catherine's death he wanted to get out there and *live,* instead of just surviving from day to day. But the object of his attentions was just about the only woman on the island who had never made a pass at him.

'Evanna? Have you been listening to a word I've been saying? Hello? Is anyone in?'

Evanna gave a start, a far-away look in her eyes as she focused on her friend. 'Sorry. Did you say something?'

'No, I'm just chatting to myself for entertainment really. I love the sound of my own voice,' Kyla quipped, rolling her eyes to the ceiling. 'I've been talking to you for *ten minutes* and you've been staring out of the window with a glazed expression on your face. If I didn't know better, I'd think I was boring.'

Evanna shook her head and gave a guilty smile. 'Sorry. I was thinking about…something.'

'Humph.' Kyla threw her a penetrating look. 'I don't suppose that *something* is six foot two, has blue eyes and shares my DNA?'

Evanna ignored the question. 'So, what were you telling me about?'

'Well, I don't have a lifetime to repeat it, so I'll just summarise,' Kyla said dryly. 'Are you going to the beach barbecue next Saturday?'

Evanna frowned. 'I'd forgotten about it.'

'How could you possibly have forgotten the highlight of the Glenmore social calendar?' Kyla sat back as Meg placed a towering ice cream in front of her. 'Thanks. I've been fantasising about this all day.'

Evanna shook her head in disbelief. 'How you can consume so much ice cream and still fit into your clothes is beyond my understanding.'

'Life is to be lived,' Kyla said airily, sticking her spoon into the ice cream. 'So—are you coming?'

Would Logan be there? Probably not, Evanna decided. He never went. And she needed to get out. *She needed the distraction.* 'I'll be there.'

'Good. Ethan and I will meet you on the beach. They're going to do a lifeboat demonstration at six.'

'Well, I refuse to be a volunteer victim.'

'We probably won't need a volunteer,' Kyla said cheerfully, finishing her ice cream in record time. 'The tourists are so reckless, one of them is bound to be drowning at the right moment.'

'Kyla, that's a terrible thing to say!'

'It's the truth. Ask the lifeboat crew. They've never been as busy as they have this summer. Is that your phone ringing?'

Evanna dug into her pocket and removed the phone. 'Missed call. I wonder who it was.' She checked the number and frowned. 'That's Sonia. I wonder what she wants. I called on her yesterday.'

'You gave her your mobile number? You're a soft touch, Evanna Duncan.' Kyla waved the spoon in her direction. 'Why don't you just let the patients move in with you? Save them having to make appointments or ring you at all.'

Evanna was too busy calling Sonia to respond. 'She isn't answering the phone.' She tried the number again but it was busy.

'She's probably busy ringing you!'

'She's supposed to be going to the hospital on Monday for a check. Her blood pressure has been giving Logan nightmares.'

Kyla's smile faded. 'Yes, well, obviously heavily pregnant

women aren't his favourite thing after what happened to Catherine.'

'I know that. But we can hardly send everyone to live on the mainland the moment they become pregnant.' Evanna glanced at her watch and stood up. 'If I go now, I've time to call in before my afternoon surgery. Thanks for the coffee. Meg?' She called across the café. 'I'm off.'

Meg was cutting a large chocolate cake into generous slices, ready for the afternoon rush. 'Will we see you at the beach barbecue, dear?'

'Yes. I hope so.' Evanna was distracted. Why was Sonia calling? Was she in trouble?

'It's going to be a fantastic night. Ben and Nick have planned the most fantastic firework display.'

'I'm looking forward to it. I'll call you, Kyla!' Evanna hurried out of the café and onto the quay. It was mid-afternoon and the sun was blazing. Tourists ambled along the pavement next to the harbour, legs and shoulders bared, feet tucked into flip-flops. They queued for boat trips and crowded into the ice-cream shops in an attempt to cool down.

'Good afternoon, Nurse Duncan!'

Spotting the headmistress from the local primary school, Evanna quickly crossed the road to talk to her.

'Hello, Miss Carne. Everything all right?' Immediately she felt ten years old again and to cover her awkwardness she stooped to pat the little dog that was panting in the heat. 'Are you enjoying the school holidays?'

'Yes. I'm off to Venice next week with my friend Diane from Glasgow. We're having a city break.'

'Well, that will be a change from island life. You have a good time and don't forget your inhalers.' She blushed, always uncomfortable discussing health topics with her old headmistress. Usually she left it to Kyla, who was much bolder.

'I won't. I had a long chat with Kyla about what I should be doing with them on holiday and Dr MacNeil wrote me a new prescription. What about you, dear? Are you getting away?'

'No. I've just had my bathroom done and it's left a hole in my bank balance.' Evanna laughed as she straightened up. 'Does that sound sad?'

'Not at all. Very indulgent. You'll be able to enjoy it the whole year round.'

'It doesn't feel indulgent at the moment when I'm stepping over dust and rubble. Still, I hope it will be finished soon.' It didn't matter how old you were, she reflected, your headmistress was always going to be your headmistress.

Miss Carne adjusted her glasses, as she'd always done at the beginning of every lesson. 'Are you going to the beach barbecue on Saturday?'

Why was everyone suddenly so interested in whether she was going? 'Yes, I think so.' Evanna brushed a strand of hair out of her eyes and tried to remind herself that she was an adult now, with a responsible job. 'Well, I'd better go. I have afternoon clinic starting soon and I want to call in on Sonia on the way.'

Miss Carne gave an indulgent smile. 'Little Evanna. You were always such a star at English.'

'But hopeless at maths,' Evanna murmured, and the other lady smiled.

'You would have done a great deal better if that little monkey Kyla hadn't always been talking to you instead of letting you concentrate! I always knew you'd be a wonderful nurse. If someone fell in the playground, you were always there, patching them up, delivering a hug.'

Evanna blushed. 'Well—it's good to see you, Miss Carne.'

'You take care, dear. Oh, Evanna—I've been meaning to ask you.' She frowned. 'Do you know the little Price girl? Helen.

She moved here in the spring with her family. She joined my reception class.'

Evanna recalled Kyla pointing out a little girl on the beach earlier in the summer. 'Vaguely. I haven't actually met them. Why?'

Ann Carne looked thoughtful. 'She just seems quite a delicate child. And I noticed during sports day that she was terribly out of breath. I thought she might have asthma.'

'Have you mentioned it to the parents?'

'Well, the father's hardly ever around. He's a journalist, I think. Travels all the time. And the mother is quite shy. Not mixing that well.'

'To my knowledge she hasn't been to see us, but obviously I was away for a month so I can't be sure. I'll dig out her records and have a check. And I'll have a word with Logan.' Evanna dodged a group of tourists and slid into her car. 'Bye, Miss Carne.'

'You shouldn't be parking there, Nurse Duncan.' Nick Hillier, the island policeman, stuck his head through her open window. 'I ought to book you.'

'Now, why would you do a thing like that when you've so many other better things to be doing?' She smiled at him, wishing that she could find him attractive. Kyla always said that it was because he'd tied their plaits together in school but Evanna knew that wasn't true. At least, not for her. The reason she couldn't find Nick Hillier attractive was because she was crazy about Logan and always had been.

'Nick, can I ask you something? When you see Miss Carne, does she make you feel as though you're back in primary school?'

He grinned. 'Every time. Even when I have her in a cell in handcuffs.'

Evanna laughed at the ridiculous image that his words created. 'I always feel very uncomfortable with her.'

'I don't know why because you were always her favourite.

In fact, you were pretty much everyone's favourite,' Nick said gruffly, and Evanna looked at him, startled.

'Nick—'

He lifted a hand and gave a rueful smile. 'I'm not going to ask you on a date because I know you'll only refuse me, and there's only so much rejection a guy can take, but are you going to the beach barbecue on Saturday?'

'Yes.' Evanna fastened her seat belt and started the engine. 'Although why everyone is so interested in whether or not I'm going is a mystery to me.'

'I suppose we're all hoping you're going to make an extra-big batch of your double chocolate brownies.' Nick grinned and stood up. 'If you don't, I just might have to give you a night in the cells handcuffed to your old headmistress.'

'If you saw the current state of my house you'd realise that the cells are currently an attractive option. I have to go, Nick. I want to call on Sonia.'

Nick frowned. 'I saw her earlier. She looked pale.'

'I'm going to check on her now.' Evanna felt a flicker of unease. 'I really have to go. Take care of yourself and make sure you arrest anyone who isn't using sun cream. We're fed up with treating burns.'

He laughed and stood back so that she could pull out.

Evanna drove away from the harbour and took the turning that led inland to Sonia's house. She should just have time to call in, reassure herself that everything was all right and that the call had been about something trivial, and still make it in time for her afternoon clinic.

And then she saw another car close behind her. An open-topped sports car with a dark-haired man at the wheel.

Logan. And he was flashing his lights.

She pulled up outside Sonia's house and hurried out of her car. 'What are you doing here? Sonia tried to phone me and—'

'Her waters have broken.' Logan's tone was grim. 'Steve called me five minutes ago. There's a ferry leaving in ten minutes. Damn it, Evanna, we'd better get her on that boat because I am not delivering another baby on this island.'

'Calm down,' Evanna said softly, reflecting on the fact that she'd never had to use those words to Logan before. In all the years they'd worked together, she'd never seen him panic. 'It's her first baby so I'm sure there's plenty of time. Given that she's only thirty-six weeks, I agree that we should transfer her to the mainland. Is she having contractions?'

'Not according to Steve.'

Evanna looked at his face and saw the tension. She put a steadying hand on his arm. 'It's going to be fine, Logan.' And then she realised what an utterly stupid thing that was to say because it hadn't been fine for Catherine. 'I'm sorry.'

'Don't be.' His voice was harsh. 'And I'm sure it will be OK but I'd rather it was fine on the mainland and not on this island. I'm not delivering another baby here, Evanna. Unless the head is actually showing, she's going on that ferry. And if the head is about to be delivered, I'm calling the helicopter.'

'Logan...' It was so unlike him to be anything other than entirely relaxed that for a moment she didn't know how to respond and she wasn't given a chance to work out the right thing to say because Steve appeared in the doorway, the phone in his hand.

'Thank goodness you're here. She's having contractions.' He spoke rapidly and there was panic in his voice. 'Strong ones. Every minute.'

Evanna grabbed her bag from the car and sprinted down the path. 'Where is she?'

'Up in the bedroom. She was having a lie-down when it all started. She stood up to go to the toilet and her waters broke. Then nothing for a while and then suddenly all this pain and she keeps yelling at me and telling me she feels sick.' Steve jabbed his fingers through his hair. 'Her bag's packed and everything. Should I take her to the hospital?'

'Yes. Get the car out of the garage,' Logan said tersely, but Evanna intervened.

'We'll just look at her first,' she said quickly, catching Logan's eye to prevent him from arguing with her. It wouldn't help Steve to know that Logan was worried. 'Can I go up?'

'Of course. You know where it is. First on the right.'

Evanna ran up the narrow staircase and pushed open the bedroom door. 'Sonia?'

She was on the floor, kneeling, her elbows on the bed. Her hair was sticking to her forehead and her eyes were scared. 'Nurse Duncan. Thank goodness. I tried to call you.'

'I know. I had a missed call and then you didn't answer. But I'm here now. Goodness, you look hot. Let's get a cool flannel on your head.' Evanna dropped her bag on the floor and knelt down next to Sonia. 'You're going to be fine, I promise. I just need to wash my hands and then I can take a look at you and we can decide what to do. Can I use the bathroom?'

'Through there.' Sonia waved a hand and then gave a howl of pain and buried her head in her arms. Steve came thundering up the stairs and slid an arm round her.

'There, love. You're doing well,' he said in a bracingly cheerful tone.

Evanna emerged from the bathroom in time to hear Sonia snap, 'Get away from me.'

Seeing the hurt and confusion on Steve's face, she put a hand on his arm. 'Women in labour always say things they don't mean,' she said softly, kneeling on the floor next to Sonia and rubbing her shoulders.

'I just want to help,' Steve said helplessly, and Evanna nodded.

'Could you fetch a jug of iced water? And a cool flannel would be welcome, I'm sure. This heat is stifling.'

'I put the fan on her but it seemed to make her cross.'

'Don't tell the whole island I'm moody!' The contraction eased and Sonia groaned. 'This is agony. Why don't any of the books tell you that it's this painful? There's all this rubbish about breathing through the pain and when it hits it's so bad I can't breathe at all!'

'How often have the pains been coming?'

'It feels continuous,' Sonia groaned. 'My waters broke and there was nothing and then suddenly, wham. Agony.'

'Evanna.' Logan's tone was sharp and Evanna looked up to see him standing in the doorway, his knuckles white as he held onto his phone. 'We need to get her to the hospital. Jim is holding the ferry.'

'I'll go and get the car,' Steve began, but at that moment Sonia turned her head and was violently sick into the bowl that Steve had left by her side.

'She can't go on a ferry like this, Logan,' Evanna remonstrated softly, sliding a hand over Sonia's shoulders to support her, 'neither can she go on a helicopter. I need to examine her, but I think she's in transition.'

'Transition?' Logan repeated the word as if he'd never heard it before, and Evanna felt a twist of unease deep inside her.

Since the death of his wife in childbirth, Logan had always been careful to transfer every woman to the mainland in time for delivery.

Was he going to be able to cope with this?

'She's not going anywhere, Logan. She's going to have the baby here, and that's fine.' For everyone's sake, Evanna kept her voice calm and steady. She didn't want to frighten Sonia. Logan's jaw tightened and he glared at her as if she were personally responsible for the fact that Sonia had gone into labour a month early while still on the island.

Understanding the reason for his tension, Evanna wanted to

reach out and hug him. *She wanted to tell him that she understood.* She wanted to reassure him and talk it through with him, but Sonia gave another groan and writhed in agony.

'Breathe in now, Sonia,' Evanna instructed, her eyes still on Logan's face as she coached Sonia through the contraction. 'That's good. Well done. Just as we practised in class.' She was talking and encouraging but her attention was on Logan.

His face was white and drawn and suddenly she felt tiny fingers of panic slide down her spine. If this turned out to be a normal delivery then there would be no problem, but if she needed a doctor, would Logan be able to help?

She'd never known him like this before—*never known him anything but completely calm and in control.* Normally it was Logan who led everything. The time Michael King had crashed his tractor and suffered a severe head injury, it had been Logan who had managed to keep him alive. When Barbara Mullond's baby had developed meningitis, it had been Logan's quick actions and incredible instincts that had prevented a disaster. He was never anything less than confident and skilled and she was used to turning to him.

As Sonia's contraction eased, Evanna rocked back on her heels and snapped on a pair of gloves.

Was it her fault? Should she have sent Sonia into hospital sooner? But even as she asked herself the question, she knew that the answer to that was no. She'd looked at the guidelines, she'd discussed Sonia's case with the hospital and she'd monitored her regularly. She'd done all the right things, but the truth was that, no matter how careful they were, childbirth was occasionally unpredictable. They couldn't transfer everyone just because they lived in a rural area.

But Logan certainly didn't need this particular outcome.

Why did life have to be so complicated? Why couldn't Sonia's delivery have been straightforward? Logan's face was white and drawn and Evanna felt awful for him, hardly daring to imagine what he must be thinking. After what had happened with Catherine, he didn't need this. And she wasn't in a position to offer the support he deserved because she had a labouring woman to deal with.

Afterwards, she promised herself, forgetting the awkwardness that had suddenly emerged between them. After this was over she'd make sure he had the opportunity to talk.

Before she could examine Sonia, another contraction consumed her and suddenly Evanna was in absolutely no doubt that the arrival of the baby was imminent. There was going to be no time to get her to the mainland. No time even to track down Ethan, the other island doctor.

Somehow she was going to have to do this by herself but make it look as though Logan was helping. *She didn't want the inhabitants of the island gossiping.*

'I don't want to do this any more! I've changed my mind.' Sonia started to sob and thump her husband. 'This is *all* your fault. All of it. I hate you. I *really* hate you. You were the one who wanted children!'

'You said you wanted them, too. Sonia...' Stricken and helpless, Steve tried to take her in his arms but she thumped his chest and pushed him away.

'Get away from me! *Don't touch me!* I hope you wanted an only child because this is the last baby we're going to have!' Sonia gave a gasp and then leaned over and vomited again.

'You poor thing,' Evanna soothed, holding the bowl and gently stroking Sonia's damp hair away from her face. 'You're in transition, Sonia. Do you remember that we talked about that stage? This is often the most uncomfortable bit of the whole process, but you're nearly there. When this contraction passes I'm going to examine you and I'm willing to bet that you're almost fully dilated and ready to push.'

Sonia's face was blotched with tears and she clutched at Evanna's hand. 'I'm scared,' she confessed, her face crumpling. 'It wasn't supposed to be like this, was it? I know it's dangerous—'

'It's not at all dangerous,' Evanna soothed, her voice calm and level. 'People have babies at home all the time. It's perfect.'

'But they don't have babies stuck on Glenmore Island! You didn't want me to have this baby at home. Dr MacNeil didn't want me to have it at home.'

'Doctors never do, but that doesn't mean that Dr MacNeil isn't perfectly capable of assisting in a delivery if he has to,' Evanna said firmly, hoping that Logan wouldn't contradict her. She slid a hand over Sonia's abdomen, feeling the tightening. 'You've got another contraction coming now, Sonia. Lovely deep breath for me.'

'It's all going wrong…'

'Everything is completely normal. Nothing is going wrong.' Evanna glanced towards Logan, willing him to say something to support her—something encouraging—but he was frozen to the spot, his face an expressionless mask. She felt her insides twist in sympathy. She could only imagine just how terrible this situation must be for him. It must bring everything back.

Perhaps some fresh air would do the trick. 'Logan.' She kept her voice light and confident. 'Can you go to the car and fetch the delivery pack from my boot, please?'

For a moment he didn't respond and she wondered if he'd even heard her. What should she do? Uneasily, she repeated her question.

'Logan—the boot's open. Can you fetch the delivery pack, please?'

'I've called the helicopter.' His voice was hoarse and Evanna gave a nod and a smile, trying to look as though they were having a routine conversation.

'That's great. Good idea. But I do need the delivery pack from my boot.' *Please,* Logan.

'Dr MacNeil?' Sonia's voice faltered and she looked pleadingly at Logan. 'Is everything all right? You look a bit funny.'

Evanna discreetly slid a hand into her pocket and removed her mobile phone. This wasn't going to work. She was going to have to call Ethan. She needed medical back-up and Logan obviously wasn't able to give it. His face was grey with strain and she hadn't seen him look so drawn since Catherine's death.

Sonia must have seen it, too, because she gave a whimper of panic. 'Dr MacNeil?'

The fear in her voice must have penetrated Logan's brain because he suddenly stepped forward. 'It's all right, Sonia.' His voice gruff, he moved across to them and sat on the edge of the bed.

Sonia's eyes were terrified. 'You don't want me to do this here, do you? You're afraid that…' The words lay unspoken in the air and Logan hesitated for a moment and then took her hand in his.

'I'm not afraid of anything,' he said roughly. 'Of course I would have rather you had the baby in hospital because I'm a doctor and we're only ever comfortable if we're surrounded by technology that beeps at us. Ask Evanna. Midwives despair of us doctors because we always try and turn childbirth into something medical because that's all we understand. But women have been having babies successfully by themselves for centuries. And Evanna is the best midwife I've ever worked with. You don't need to worry.'

Almost weak with relief, Evanna slid the phone back into her pocket without making the call. 'Well, luckily for you, I'm here to show you how it's supposed to be done, Dr MacNeil,' she said lightly. 'But in order to do that, I need some equipment.'

'Of course. The delivery pack from your boot.' Logan gave Sonia's hand another squeeze and rose to his feet. 'I'll fetch it.'

He left the room and Sonia screwed up her face. 'Oh, here we go again. Oh, my...' She swore fluently and her husband blinked several times and then glanced at Evanna, embarrassment on his face.

'I've never heard her use language like that before.'

'Don't worry about it.'

'My feet are tingling. Something's the matter.'

'You're breathing too fast, that's what's the matter,' Evanna said calmly. 'Just try and slow everything down. That's better. Good. Here's Dr MacNeil now. I'm going to wash my hands, then I'm going to examine you.'

'Don't leave me!' Sonia's voice was sharp with panic. 'Please, don't leave me!'

'I'm just going to—'

'I want to push.'

Logan opened the pack swiftly, his hands steady. 'She can't possibly have dilated that quickly,' he muttered to Evanna, and she cast a wry smile in his direction.

'Babies don't always perform according to the textbook. Don't push, Sonia, because if you're not fully dilated you could damage your cervix. Steve, can you fetch clean towels and spread them over the floor?' Swiftly Evanna washed her hands and pulled on a pair of gloves.

Sonia was trying to breathe steadily. 'My back hurts so much. I'm so uncomfortable.'

Evanna looked at Steve who had returned with armfuls of towels, which he placed at Sonia's feet. 'If you could just rub her lower back, that might help.' She quickly checked her equipment and prepared for the delivery. A swift examination told her that there was no time to move Sonia even had she wanted to. Her perineum was distended and the head was clearly visible. 'This baby is certainly in a hurry. I can see the baby's head, Sonia, so I don't need to examine you. Try and relax between contractions. That's good. Now pant. Don't push. Pant.' As she delivered the baby's head she was aware of Logan beside her and felt relieved to have him there.

'Cord,' he said quietly, and she gave a nod and gently freed the loop of cord that was round the baby's neck. 'I'll give the syntometrine. I don't think we should risk a physiological third stage. Do you agree?'

It was typical of Logan to confer with her rather than just dictating, as so many other doctors would have done in the same situation. Evanna nodded agreement, knowing that to leave the placenta to be delivered naturally increased the chances of post-partum haemorrhage. And they had no facilities to deal with haemorrhage.

'One more push and the baby should be born, Sonia,' she said huskily, hoping and praying that this was one delivery that would be straightforward from here on. *Please, don't let there be any complications.* Not this time. Not again. Glenmore Island had already had its fair share of obstetric emergencies.

The baby shot out into her waiting hands and Evanna let out a delighted laugh that was full of relief. 'Oh, Sonia, she's beautiful. A little girl.' The baby yelled furiously and Sonia gave a sob as she turned onto her bottom and took the baby from Evanna.

'Oh, Steve.' Sonia's voice was choked and tears poured down her face as she held her daughter. 'She's beautiful. Perfect.'

Evanna looked at Logan, saw him dispose of the syringe and close his eyes briefly. Then he caught her gaze and gave a faint smile and a nod.

'OK.'

'OK,' Evanna agreed quietly, as she clamped the cord. 'A perfectly straightforward delivery. Thank you, Dr MacNeil.'

'I didn't—'

'You were great. Sonia, I think you'd be more comfortable up on the bed now. You can have a proper cuddle with her.'

Kyla appeared in the doorway. 'I gather we're having a drama. The helicopter is here. Oh, my goodness, they're obviously a bit late.' She watched as Evanna delivered the placenta and then she grinned at Sonia. 'You were always determined to have your home birth, weren't you?'

Sonia shook her head, her eyes misty. 'It was perfect. I wouldn't have missed a moment of it.'

'Perfect? Are you kidding?' Steve stared at her in confusion. 'You were yelling like a madwoman. And telling me we were never having any more children. And swearing.'

'Was I?' Placid and calm now, Sonia gently stroked the baby's head. 'She needs a bath. And so do I. It's so hot in here. Why did I have to have a baby in August? Next time I'm going for January.'

Quietly, and with a minimum of fuss, Evanna helped Sonia attach the baby to the breast, skin to skin, and then covered her. 'It will help your uterus contract,' she explained, 'and also keep the baby warm.' She looked at Logan. *Saw the lines of strain around his eyes.* 'She needs to go to the hospital anyway, given that her blood pressure was up and the baby is four weeks early. We may as well use your helicopter.'

He nodded agreement. 'I'll go and speak to them. Will you get her ready?'

'She's a month early.' Sonia was watching the feeding baby with wonder and awe. 'Will she be all right?'

'Well, if her appetite is anything to go by, she's going to fit right into this island. We'll have her gorging herself at Meg's in no time,' Kyla said with a grin, helping Evanna to clear up. 'What are you calling her?'

'Oh...' Sonia glanced at Steve, her eyes shining. 'We couldn't agree, could we? It was a battle between Emma and Rachel.'

'You wanted Rachel and I think she looks like a Rachel,' Steve murmured, his voice gruff. 'What do you think of Rachel Evanna?'

Touched, Evanna glanced up from her preparations. 'You don't have to do that.'

'We want to.' Sonia smiled at her husband and then looked at Evanna, gratitude in her eyes. 'We're so grateful to you and Dr MacNeil. You were both amazing.'

'Just don't call her Logan,' Kyla advised cheerfully, folding a towel neatly. 'One of those is more than enough on an island this size. I'll go and tell the helicopter lads what's happening. Which one of you is going with her?'

'Me,' Evanna said immediately. 'Logan has to get back to surgery and then there's Kirsty to think of. Can you cover my clinic, Kyla? Ask some of them to come back tomorrow.'

'I don't think they'll mind doing that, given the reason.' Kyla took a last peep at the baby and sighed. 'Maybe I'm broody after all.'

Evanna laughed and ignored the painful twist of her heart. 'I'd better warn Ethan.'

CHAPTER EIGHT

LOGAN'S house was in darkness.

Could he already be in bed? She was later than she'd planned, but by the time she'd sorted Sonia out and completed all the paperwork, several hours had passed. Reluctant to knock on the front door in case she woke Kirsty, Evanna walked round the back of the house and opened the garden gate.

She'd just take a look. If there were no lights on then she'd give up and go home. But she wasn't comfortable about just going home.

Not until she'd checked on Logan. The whole experience must have been completely harrowing for him and she wanted to give him a chance to talk about it. But there was no sign of life in the house. Just one small light burning in the hall.

Could he be out?

Perhaps he'd found a babysitter and gone down to the pub to celebrate the birth of Rachel Evanna, along with the rest of the locals.

She walked into his garden, intending to look through the back door, but then she spotted him sprawled in the hammock at the end of the garden. The moon provided just enough light for her to see that he was holding a bottle of beer in his hand.

'Logan?' Perhaps he didn't want to be disturbed. It was a

stiflingly warm summer's evening, but his garden was cooled by a breeze drifting in from the sea. It was peaceful and tranquil and the perfect setting for quiet contemplation. And she was fairly sure that she knew what he was thinking about. Or who.

Catherine.

Feeling like an intruder and wishing she'd never come, Evanna was just wondering whether to melt back through the garden gate and into her car when he spoke.

'I thought you'd be in the pub with the others.' His voice was low and impossibly sexy and she walked across to him on shaking legs, wondering why she continued to torture herself like this.

'I wasn't in the mood for celebrations.'

'Why not?' He lifted the bottle and drank. 'You did a good job.'

'So did you.'

'Me?' His mouth twisted into a smile and his blue eyes glittered with an emotion that she didn't recognise. 'You did all the work, Evanna.'

'I'm the midwife. I'm supposed to do all the work. If you'd taken over, I would have resigned on the spot. Goodness knows, I get little enough opportunity to deliver babies on this island—that's why I go to the mainland once a year. Otherwise I'd forget how to do it.' She kept her tone light and then sighed. 'All right, let's stop being tactful and be honest. I was worried about you. That's why I'm here. It must have been completely hideous to have to cope with that. I can't even begin to imagine—and I wasn't able to give you any support because of Sonia, and all the time I knew that you were in agony and I just wanted to give you a hug. So I'm here to check you're all right.' The words tumbled out of her and she felt horribly self-conscious. They hadn't had a proper talk since he'd caught her coming out of the shower and their whole relationship seemed to have changed since then. What if he didn't want to talk to her any more?

What if things were different?

He stirred and the hammock swung gently. 'I'm sorry if I gave you a fright back there. You needed support and I wasn't any help at all.'

'That's not true,' Evanna said quickly. 'You were great.'

He gave a twisted smile that was loaded with derision. 'I froze. If you hadn't given me that look, I probably would have just turned and run. Yesterday was the first time in my entire medical career that I panicked.'

'And is that really so surprising? No one who had been through what you went through would have found that situation anything other than difficult.'

There was a long silence and then he put the empty bottle down on the grass and stretched out a hand. 'Come and sit down.'

Evanna eyed the swaying hammock. 'In that?'

'Of course. There's plenty of room for two.'

'That's when one of the two is a toddler.'

'Just be careful how you climb in or you'll tip me out.' He closed his fingers over her wrist and gave her a gentle tug so that she tumbled off balance and landed on top of him.

'Logan!' Thoroughly embarrassed, she rolled off him and lay on her back in the hammock. They were hip to hip, shoulder to shoulder and, for a moment, she couldn't breathe. Then she looked up and gave a murmur of delight. 'Oh—the stars are amazing.'

'You've never lain in this at night?'

'You know I haven't.'

'It's so hot indoors that I'd sleep here at the moment if it weren't for Kirsty. So why did you come, Evanna?'

His quiet question flustered her. 'I wanted to check on you.'

'I'm not one of your patients.'

'I—' *What did he want her to say?* 'I know that. But I care about you.'

'And that's why you wanted to hug me?' He turned to look

at her, a dangerous glitter in his blue eyes. 'Because you care about me? You care about everyone, Evanna. You always have. At school you were the one who broke up fights, smoothed everyone's feathers. You always hated conflict. Caring is part of your personality.'

His face was close to hers. *So close.* Evanna's heart lurched. Had he guessed how she felt about him? Had she failed to hide it? 'Of course I care about you.' Her voice came out as a whisper, as if anything else would have punctured the perfect stillness of the garden. 'We all care about you, Logan.'

For a moment he didn't respond and it seemed to her that the air around them thickened with tension. 'So the whole community is still keeping an eye on me.'

'You make it sound patronising, but it isn't like that.'

'Isn't it?'

'No.' *His eyelashes were really long.* And dark. Such a contrast to his blue eyes. 'You're not an object of pity, if that's what you mean. No one could ever pity you because you're so strong, but that doesn't stop them feeling sad for you or wanting to protect you from any more pain. The situation with Sonia this afternoon must bring it all back and that must be hard.' She felt the hard muscle of his leg brush against hers and felt crazy flutters of excitement in her stomach.

'What's hard is realising that I'm nothing like people's image of me.' There was a harshness in his tone that disturbed her.

'What do you mean?'

He gave a faint smile. 'People look at me and see a dedicated doctor. Grieving widower. Single father. Doting dad.'

'I suppose. Maybe. Aren't you all those things?'

He stared at her for a long moment and then dragged his eyes away and stared up at the sky. 'Am I?'

He was frustratingly uncommunicative. 'What are you

thinking? You're obviously upset. Talk to me,' she urged, and he gave a cynical laugh.

'You know that men aren't great at talking.'

'But you are. When you want to be. I've seen you spend hours with patients who are worried about something. You're amazingly intuitive and a fantastic listener.'

'Not such a great talker.'

Evanna swallowed. 'You've always talked to me.'

'That's true. Funny, that, isn't it? I've said things to you that I've never said aloud before.' There was a long, throbbing silence and then he turned to look at her again. 'The truth is that I'm not feeling what I'm expected to feel.'

'I don't think anyone expects anything, Logan.'

'Don't they? I'm supposed to be devastated and far too grief-ridden to even contemplate—' He broke off, swore softly and ran a hand over his face. 'I think of Catherine, that's true, but lately…'

'Lately?'

He paused and then reached across and took her hand in his. 'Lately—well, let's just say that lately a lot of things have changed.'

Evanna didn't know whether to snatch her hand away or hold on tight. It felt impossibly intimate to be lying together in the dark, touching, even if she knew that, for him, that touch was only a symbol of friendship.

The air around them was still and the heat was stifling, despite the lateness of the hour. They were enclosed by the garden and the silence of a summer evening, disturbed only by the faint barking of a dog from the farm across the fields.

Reminding herself that the whole point of coming up here that evening was to listen to him, she forced herself to ignore the firm press of his fingers against hers. 'What's changed, Logan?' She struggled to sound casual and Logan gave a short laugh.

'I have. I've changed.'

'Well, I'm sure that's to be expected. No one could go through what you went through and not change. And I don't think that there's a right and a wrong to cope with anything. You just have to do what feels right for you. We all struggle through life in the best way we can, and you do brilliantly.'

'Do I? Tell me, Evanna, what is the required time for remaining celibate after the loss of a wife? A year? Two years? More?'

'I've never thought about it.' Startled by the question, she hoped that the darkness hid the sudden rush of colour to her cheeks. 'I suppose it depends on the individual. You're a normal, healthy guy, Logan, and surely it's to be expected that you'd— I mean of course eventually you're going to— It's natural to—'

'Want sex?' He didn't let go of her hand. 'Is it? Is it natural to be interested in another woman? To be honest, the feeling took me by surprise.'

Was he telling her that he wanted to have sex with someone?

Her heart flipped and she struggled to squash down the sick feeling of disappointment that rose up inside her. This wasn't about her, she reminded herself swiftly, this was about him. Of course he was going to want sex. He was a healthy adult male in his prime. 'You're telling me that you're interested in other women? I think that's...' She hesitated over the word. 'Great,' she said firmly. 'Really great. It means you're moving on.'

'Does it?'

'Of course.'

He turned his head to look at her. 'You're not shocked?'

'That you want a relationship? Of course not. I'm thrilled for you.'

His mouth moved into a slow smile. 'I didn't say I wanted a relationship,' he murmured softly. 'That might be more complicated. I'm just talking about sex.'

'Oh—yes, of course.' Suddenly flustered, Evanna struggled

for the right thing to say. 'Well, I think that—that it's fine. Whatever works for you. More than anyone, you deserve happiness, Logan.' Despite the darkness, she could feel him watching her.

'You're so sweet. And generous.' His voice was soft and his hand held hers firmly. 'You never judge, do you?'

She mustn't mind that he thought she was sweet. Sweet was a compliment, she told herself firmly. 'What is there to judge?'

'Plenty of people would.'

'And does that bother you?'

He gave a soft laugh. 'What do you think?'

'I think that you've never minded what people say about you. You've always done your own thing and, frankly, that's the only way to be able to live on an island this size. So what's the problem?' She tried to put her own feelings aside and respond in the way that she would have done had she not been emotionally involved. 'Is there someone you like? Someone special? Obviously there must be, or you wouldn't have suddenly started thinking about…sex.' She tried to sound relaxed, as if conversations about sex were an everyday occurrence for her. He wanted to talk about it, she told herself, and she should allow him that. It was the least she could do.

The darkness of the garden folded over them, creating an atmosphere of intimacy that seemed to mock her. Here she was, lying in the darkness, on a perfect summer's evening, holding hands with the man she loved while he told her about another woman that interested him.

'Maybe. I don't know. I'm in dangerous territory.'

'Because you feel guilty about Catherine?'

'Strangely enough, no. I don't feel guilty. I probably should, but I don't. If there's one thing that I learned from Catherine, it's that life is to be lived.'

'That's true.' Evanna smiled. 'She was a very adventurous

person. A bit wild. If she were standing here now, she'd probably just want to know why it's taken you so long. So, if you don't feel guilty and you're not worried about what anyone thinks, why is it dangerous territory? What's holding you back?'

He was looking at her and he still hadn't let go of her hand. 'Because I'm not sure that the woman in question is interested in me.'

'Logan MacNeil, I never heard such nonsense! Women have been falling over you since you first learned to walk. And you've never been one to hold back! Just ask her!'

'You think I should ask a woman for sex?'

Evanna laughed to hide her embarrassment. 'I think you might need to be a little more subtle than that or someone might slap your face.'

'So what should I do?'

Just smile, she wanted to say. That's all it would take in her case. One smile and she'd be his for ever. 'Give her one of your hot looks! I don't know, you're the expert,' she mumbled. 'If ever a man knew how to put the moves on a woman, it was you. There were more broken hearts in our school than in a coronary care unit.'

He smiled at her analogy. 'That was a long time ago. In my wild, reckless youth.'

Despite the humour in his tone, she decided not to point out that he'd still been breaking hearts up to the day before he'd met Catherine, which had only been two years previously. 'Well, I'm sure it's like riding a bicycle,' Evanna joked weakly. 'Just get back out there. Go for it. There are no end of possible candidates. Loads of women who aren't your patients. Polly in the pub. She's very pretty. Or Mary Simon, who helps Meg in the café. Any woman would want to be asked out by you.'

He didn't release her hand. 'Would they?'

His thigh was pressed hard against hers.

'Of course.' His features seemed dark and unfamiliar and she swallowed hard. 'What do you think?'

It was a moment before he answered. 'I think that sometimes when something is incredibly familiar, we don't always notice it. We think something is a certain way and then suddenly we discover that we were entirely wrong. And that takes some adjustment.'

He was talking in riddles. Her eyes slid to the empty bottle on the ground but it was a small bottle and there was only the one so it couldn't be that. And, anyway, she hadn't known Logan to drink to excess since that one occasion on the beach on his seventeenth birthday when she and Kyla had spent an entire night holding his head over a bowl while he'd been sick. 'You think Polly and Mary don't notice you? Because I can tell you now that they—'

'I'm not talking about Polly or Mary.' His gaze was steady on hers and her stomach performed a series of elaborate acrobatics.

Determined not to read something into his words that wasn't there, she kept her tone matter-of-fact. 'Well, if you're suggesting that people see you as a widower and not as a man, I don't think that's true, Logan. If you're interested in someone then you should just go for it.'

'You think so? You think I should go for it?'

'Definitely.' She ignored the new surge of misery that flooded through her veins. Here she was, advising the man she loved to go out and find another woman. But he deserved happiness and so did Kirsty. And he deserved a sex life. But it was impossible not to feel envious of the woman who was going to find herself burning up the sheets with Logan. 'Find the right moment and go for it.'

His eyes dropped to her mouth and for a wild, crazy moment she really thought he was going to kiss her. She even found herself leaning towards him.

And then she remembered her promise to herself, snatched her hand from his and struggled out of the hammock, almost twisting her ankle and landing flat on her bottom in the process. 'It isn't easy to stand up from one of these with dignity,' she said in a strangled voice, horrified to realise just how close she'd come to kissing him.

'Evanna, you don't have to—'

'I should really be going,' she said in a bright voice. 'I mean, I just came to check up on you. And you should be going. Inside, I mean. Because you can't go anywhere because you're already here. Obviously.' Nerves made her babble incoherently and she almost groaned as she listened to herself.

What must he think of her?

No wonder he didn't find her sexy. She didn't have the first clue about seducing men.

Logan simply watched her, his handsome face unsmiling. 'So that's it? You're leaving?'

What did he expect? Did he want her to pull out a pad and pen and start drawing up a list of possible candidates for his sexual pleasure?

'It's late.' She waved a hand in the vague direction of the gate. 'I should be going, and you should be—'

He scooped up the empty bottle and stood up in a smooth, athletic movement that was a complete contrast to her own tumbled exit from the hammock. 'I should be getting back to the woman in my life. My daughter.'

There was an awkward silence and Evanna chewed her lip, wishing that she was better at talking about sex. Kyla would have lain there and chatted quite comfortably about any topic of his choice, but she'd been gauche and stiff.

'I haven't helped much, have I?' she mumbled, and for a long moment Logan didn't answer.

Then he gave a sigh. 'You always help. Thanks for coming

round, Evanna,' he said gruffly, and she gave a helpless nod as she backed towards the garden gate.

'You're welcome. I'm sorry I didn't— I mean, I hope it works out the way you want,' she muttered, and then gave up trying to say the right thing and just made for her car.

Find the right moment.
Find the right moment.

Logan paced the floor of his bedroom, battling with a growing frustration. Hadn't that been Evanna's advice to him? But when exactly was the right moment to tell a woman that you wanted to strip her naked and have wild, abandoned sex with her?

Evanna's life was so tidy and neat. Everything planned. He'd seen the way that she'd blushed when he'd mentioned sex. How much deeper would that blush have been had she known that the woman he was interested in was her?

Any other woman would have picked up his signals, but not Evanna.

Evanna didn't do wild love affairs and she never had.

She was sweet and conservative and a bit shy. The sort of woman who blushed when she was caught coming out of the shower.

And, as far as he was concerned, that just made her all the more appealing.

They'd been sitting in the dark in his garden, talking about life. Talking about the future. Surely there would never be a better moment to tell a woman that you were interested in her, and yet had he spoken up? No. He'd lain there like a tongue-tied, hormonal teenager on a first date. Dropping hints. Skirting around the subject.

Logan walked over to the window and stared out over the garden.

He hadn't really thought about sex for a year and suddenly

he couldn't think about anything else. But there was only one woman that interested him. And he had absolutely no idea how to go about telling her. And this lack of confidence with the female sex was an entirely new experience for him.

Never in his life could he recall being anything less than confident with a woman. He'd seen. He'd wanted. He'd taken. It had all come so easily to him.

But Evanna was different.

He ran a hand over his face and sat back in his chair. There was so much more at stake than rejection and damage to his ego. If he got this wrong then a lifelong friendship would be damaged. Glenmore was a small, close-knit community. If it all went wrong, they wouldn't be able to avoid each other. It could be hideously awkward.

Was it really worth the risk?

Given the choice of Evanna as a friend or Evanna out of his life, which would he choose?

Without question, he'd rather keep her as a friend than lose her. Which meant that he now found himself in an extremely delicate situation.

He'd just have to work harder at forgetting her, he promised himself, sprawling on the bed without any expectation of actually sleeping.

Somehow, he'd get their relationship back to the place where it had always been.

'I've got Jenny Price in Reception with Helen.' Janet's voice was crisp and efficient on the phone. 'Can you fit her in?'

Helen Price. 'Well, that's a bit spooky because I promised Ann Carne I'd take a look at her notes this week.' Evanna ran through the conversation in her head. 'Send them in, of course. Do you know what the problem is?'

'No. But Jenny Price is very quiet. Shy. Keeps herself to

herself. But she looks worried and there's something about that child that doesn't seem right to me.'

Evanna tucked the phone between her shoulder and her ear so that she could finish printing off the letter she was writing. 'What's that?'

'That child is small.'

Evanna took the paper out of the printer and sighed, remembering Ann's concerns. 'She's five years old, Janet. Little girls of five are often delicate.'

'Maybe. Maybe not.'

Evanna smiled. 'OK, I'll take a look. If I'm worried, I'll get Logan to examine her. Is he still around or has he gone out on calls?' She'd successfully avoided him all week and buried herself in work, trying not to think that he might be out there seducing one incredibly lucky woman.

'He's just finishing his list.'

'Send in Jenny and Helen whenever they're ready.' They appeared at her door only moments later.

Jenny was a slender, nervous-looking woman with mousy hair caught up in a clip at the back of her head. She looked pale and harassed. 'Nurse Duncan, I know I should have made an appointment, but—'

'It really doesn't matter at all, Mrs Price.' Evanna interrupted her apology with a dismissive wave of her hand and a friendly smile. 'We try to be quite informal on Glenmore if we can.'

Jenny pulled a face. 'Where I was living last you were lucky to be able to get an appointment within a fortnight.'

'By which time you're either dead or cured.' Evanna smiled with understanding and brought up Helen's notes on the computer. 'How can we help you today?'

Jenny hesitated and then glanced towards her daughter. 'It isn't anything specific. Well, I suppose it is in a way. I mean, she gets incredibly breathless when she runs around and that's starting to worry me because a young girl of her age surely shouldn't be that unfit.'

'So she's breathless. Anything else?'

'Well, we had a terrible winter with chest infections.' Jenny bit her lip. 'I'm wondering whether it could be asthma. That's why I came to see you because Miss Carne, the headmistress, told me that you and the other nurse see patients with asthma.'

'Yes, we do, although in the first instance patients are diagnosed by one of the doctors. Then we usually do the follow-up and make any adjustments to medication.'

Helen wandered over to Jenny and tugged at her sleeve. 'Mummy, I'm thirsty.' She was a small, pale girl with soft blonde hair and delicate features.

Evanna watched her for a moment, remembering what both Ann and Janet had said. 'I'll fetch you a glass of water, Helen,' she said gently, walking over to the brightly coloured paper cups she kept for children. 'Can you just step on the scales for me?'

She weighed Helen, recorded the result and then handed her a cup of chilled water. Then she questioned Jenny in more depth, asking her about Helen's medical history.

'She was a normal delivery. No problems. Since then she's had chest infections. Every winter she starts. Nasty cough.'

'Does she cough at night?'

'Not in the summer. Only when she has an infection.'

'And have you ever seen a doctor about her infections?'

'Every winter we end up at the doctor's but they just say that chest infections are normal in winter.' She gave a shrug. 'But I know there's something wrong. When you're a mother you have a sense about these things. An instinct.'

Evanna glanced towards the little girl but she was playing happily with the basket of toys in the corner of the room, apparently oblivious to the conversation. 'And you say that she's out of breath the whole time.'

'I've watched her playing with other kids. She's different. She's just so out of breath when she runs around,' Jenny said quietly. 'And it seems to be getting worse.'

Could it be asthma? 'Has she ever suffered from eczema?' Evanna asked a series of questions and then stood up. 'I'm going to see if one of our doctors is available to see her.'

She lifted the phone and spoke to Janet who told her that Logan was with his last patient. She waited for his light to flash on and tapped on his door.

'I wondered if you could see a patient for me.' She was trying desperately to think of him as a doctor and not as a man. *A man who was currently fantasising about some unknown but incredibly fortunate woman.*

'Who is it?'

'Helen Price. They moved into the Garrett property in the spring. She's extremely breathless on exertion. Funnily enough, Ann Carne mentioned her to me. She wondered if she was asthmatic and the mother thinks that, too, but—'

'But you don't think so.'

'Well, obviously you need to take a look at her but, no, I'm not sure about asthma. There's no family history of atopy, no wheezing and no night cough. On the other hand, she is getting chest infections every winter.' Evanna broke off and gave an apologetic smile. 'Look, you're the doctor. I just have a funny feeling about her.'

'Then I'll see her, of course. Send her in.' His eyes lingered on hers. 'Why don't you stay while I examine her?'

Evanna nodded. 'I'll do that. And I think we ought to invite Jenny, the mother, to the beach barbecue. Her husband works away a lot and I think she's a bit lonely. Janet doesn't think she's really settled into island life.'

'Invite her. Good idea.'

'Are you going?' She didn't know what made her ask the

question. He didn't usually go. And she shouldn't care whether he was going or not.

He studied her face, his blue eyes speculative. 'Probably.'

And suddenly Evanna wished that she hadn't asked the question. Of course he'd be going. Why hadn't she thought of that? The beach barbecue would be the perfect opportunity to deepen his relationship with the woman he fancied. And that was good, she told herself firmly. Last year he hadn't attended and she'd spent the entire evening worrying about him, alone in his beautiful big house with a six-month-old baby for company. She'd left early and taken him a plate of food and they'd sat in his garden, chatting about all sorts of things. Normal things. *Things designed to distract him from the death of his wife.*

'I'm glad you're going.' She braced herself and smiled. 'Everyone will be thrilled to see you there.' She backed towards the door, wondering why he was studying her so intently. 'I'll just fetch Helen and her mother.'

When she returned, Logan was thorough and professional, questioning Jenny in detail and then examining the little girl.

Finally he unhooked the stethoscope from his ears and gave a brief smile as he handed Helen a colouring book and crayons. 'Do you want to colour that for me, Helen? I just need to talk to your mum.'

Helen grabbed the book with a delighted smile and a mumbled, 'Thank you,' and immediately lay on her stomach on the floor and started colouring.

Logan sat back down at his desk. 'Has anyone ever mentioned to you that she has a murmur?'

'A murmur?' Jenny stared at him. 'You mean a heart murmur?'

'That's right.' Logan's voice was quiet as he tucked the stethoscope into his pocket. 'When I'm using the stethoscope on her chest I'm listening to the sounds that her heart makes. A heart murmur is basically an extra sound.'

'Are you telling me that you think she has something wrong with her heart? Oh, my gosh.' Jenny's face drained of colour and she lifted a hand to her mouth. 'How can you possibly know that from just listening?'

'I don't know, for sure. And a number of young children would be found to have heart murmurs and yet have structurally normal hearts. But given her history of breathlessness and the fact that her weight is lower than average for her age, I'd like to refer her for some more tests. I think we do need to check this out further.'

'I thought it was asthma,' Jenny whispered. 'She gets all these chest infections.'

'Yes. I read that in her notes.'

'No one ever mentioned her heart before. Are you saying that chest infections can be linked to heart disease?' Jenny's eyes were wide. 'What exactly do you think is wrong?'

Logan hesitated. 'It's impossible for me to give a definitive diagnosis just by listening to her chest. I'd like you to go to the mainland and see the paediatric cardiologist. He'll do an echocardiogram, which will allow him to look at the structure of the heart. He'll also probably do a chest X-ray and an ECG, to see how the heart is working. All of that is non-invasive and won't hurt Helen at all.'

'I can't believe this.' Jenny ran a hand across her face and took several deep breaths. 'I...' She struggled with tears and Evanna reached across to borrow Logan's phone.

'Janet?' She quickly spoke to the receptionist. 'Can you come and take Helen and show her some interesting toys, please? It's very boring in here for her and she's finished the colouring Logan gave her.'

Jenny shot her a grateful look and moments later Janet appeared, a wide smile on her motherly features. 'You come with your Aunty Janet. I've all the plants to water and I really need some help,' she said happily, holding out a hand to Helen, who scrambled to her feet and glanced towards her mother doubtfully.

'You go, sweetie,' Jenny breathed, her smile just a little forced. 'Help Janet with the plants. Then Mummy will come and get you.'

Helen slipped her hand into Janet's and went without protest.

Jenny reached into her bag for a tissue. 'That was kind of you,' she whispered, blowing her nose hard. 'You try so hard to protect them, don't you? And then something like this happens. I'm sorry to be a baby, but it's such a shock.'

'I can understand that.' Logan's voice was kind, his gaze sympathetic. 'But I'd really like you to try not to worry until you know exactly what there is to worry about. That's easier said than done, I know, because once you're a parent all hope of being calm and rational goes out of the window.'

'Do you have children?'

Logan gave a crooked smile. 'Little girl. Thirteen months. So I know all about parental worry.'

'Oh. Yes.' Jenny blew her nose again. 'So what happens now?'

'I'd like to ring a good friend of mine who is a paediatric cardiologist. He'll arrange for you to have those tests that I described. Then you come back to me and we'll talk.'

'But you definitely think there's something wrong with her heart.'

'Yes, I do,' Logan said quietly, 'and I'm not going to lie to you about that. But she's a bonny little girl who has obviously done very well up until now. This may be something that is easily solved. They may even decide to wait and do nothing.'

Jenny was still struggling with tears. 'My husband, Bobbie, is away so I can't even talk to him.'

Logan leaned forward and covered her hand with his. 'You can talk to us,' he said gruffly, glancing towards Evanna. 'Anything. Any time.'

Jenny gave a dismissive laugh. 'You're suggesting I make an appointment just to discuss how worried I am about my daughter's heart?'

'Yes. Why wouldn't you? Being a GP is about caring for the whole family.' Logan's eyes were kind. 'Let's have those tests done and then talk again. If there are any decisions to be made, I'll help you weigh up all the pros and cons.'

'You're incredibly kind.' Janet shook her head. 'I—I'm just not used to having a GP who encourages me to come back. The practice we were in before had eighteen GPs. I never saw the same person twice and they were never interested in anything other than hurrying me out of the door as fast as possible.'

Logan nodded. 'Different pace of life,' he said easily, 'and different priorities. Glenmore is a small community, Jenny. And when you moved here, you became part of that. I'm going to call the cardiologist now and I'll phone you with an appointment time. Will you be able to get her to the mainland?'

'Oh, yes, I have a car and I travel across once a week anyway, to see my sister.'

'Good. Here's my home number and my mobile.' Logan scribbled on a piece of paper. 'Call me if you need to. Otherwise I'll see you when we have some results.'

Jenny slipped the piece of paper into her bag and stood up. 'Thank you.' She looked at Evanna and gave a faltering smile. 'And thank you, too.'

'You're very welcome.'

Evanna took Jenny to find her daughter and then returned to Logan. 'You really think she has a heart defect?'

'Yes. But obviously it needs to be confirmed by the cardiologist. She needs an echo.'

Evanna looked at him. 'But now that it's just you and me—tell me what you think.'

He didn't hesitate. 'I think she has an ASD. Atrial septal

defect.' He was sure and confident. 'The second heart sound is split. It's fairly characteristic.'

'But why hasn't it been picked up before now?'

'There are often no symptoms in early childhood. But in Helen's case I'm fairly sure that her breathlessness, the chest infections and the fact that her weight is below the tenth percentile...' He shrugged. 'I could be wrong.'

'You're not usually wrong, Logan,' Evanna murmured, and he studied her for a long moment.

'Are you leading my fan club?'

'You're a good doctor. You don't need me to tell you that. So what will they do? Surgery? Or did I read somewhere that they sometimes close on their own?'

'It's unlikely that Helen's will close on its own. By the time a child has reached the age of three it's extremely unlikely that it will sort itself out, and she's five and a half.'

'Which means surgery, then.'

'Not necessarily. There are some new techniques that can be done by an interventional cardiologist, rather than a surgeon. Basically they attach a device to a catheter and they can put it in place without having to stop the heart.'

Evanna pulled a face. 'Which still sounds scary when it's a child. Poor Jenny. And her husband away, too. How quickly can you get her an appointment?'

'I'm going to call him now.' Logan opened a file on the computer and scrolled down a list of phone numbers. 'We worked together in London and he's a really bright guy. I'm hoping he can fit her in this week. Did you call the hospital about Sonia?'

'Yes. They're very happy with her. Baby is a bit jaundiced so they're going to keep her in for a few days but they hope she'll be home by the middle of the week.'

'A good outcome, then.' Logan reached for the phone and

then looked at her. 'You asked me about the beach barbecue, but what about you? Are you going?'

Did she want to spend the evening watching him with another woman? The answer was very definitely no, but to not go would draw attention to herself. And anyway she lived on an island. No matter how she felt about Logan, she had to get on with her life. 'I'm going.'

The beach was big enough, she reassured herself. There would be volleyball and football and a barbecue going, not to mention swimming. It should be easy enough not to have to stand staring at him.

CHAPTER NINE

EVANNA spent Saturday afternoon getting ready for the beach barbecue in her new bathroom. She opened the windows and lay in a deep bubble bath, soaking away the stresses of the week and enjoying the view of the sea. There couldn't be many people lucky enough to have a view of the sea from their bathroom, she thought to herself when she finally eased herself out of the suds and reached for a towel.

She dried her hair and put on her bikini, knowing that the evening usually began with a swim. The she pulled on a halter-neck sundress in a deep shade of blue and slid her feet into pretty flip-flops. There was no point in considering elaborate footwear when she knew from experience that she'd be spending most of the evening barefoot.

Her doorbell rang just as she was pushing a towel into a raffia bag.

It was Kyla. 'Ethan and I thought we'd give you a lift.'

Evanna picked up her key and pulled the door closed. 'How many people are coming, do you know?'

'Everyone. How's Sonia—have you heard?'

They walked to the car and Evanna smiled at Ethan who was lounging in the driver's seat, a pair of dark glasses shielding his eyes. 'Sonia is doing very well.' She squashed into the back seat of Ethan's sports car. 'She came out on Wednesday and I've already seen her in Meg's, chatting to Lucy and feeding the baby.'

'Those two will have a lot in common. Quite nice, really.' Kyla checked her lipstick in the mirror. 'A sort of ready-made support group. And how was Logan? I expected him to be traumatised but he's actually seemed quite buoyant all week.'

Evanna fastened her seat belt. And she knew why that was. He was thinking about a woman. 'He seems fine. He looked pretty grey to start with but then he seemed to pull himself together and he was fine during the delivery.'

'Really?'

'He's fine,' Ethan drawled, pulling up in a vacant parking space. 'You girls worry too much.'

They arrived at the beach, parked in the car park and then made their way down the steps to the sand. A delicious smell of charcoal and cooking floated through the air and a group of teenagers were playing an extremely noisy game of volleyball on the sand.

Automatically, Evanna wandered over to help with the food.

'We're all under control,' Meg said firmly, giving her a gentle push. 'You go and have a swim, dear. It's so hot, I'm sure you need it.'

'I must admit, I do fancy a swim. Are you sure you can manage here?'

'Absolutely. If I need help, I'll yell. Kyla and Ethan are already in, look.' She adjusted her sunglasses. 'Go and join them.'

Deciding that it was too hot to argue, Evanna wriggled out of her dress, folded it neatly and placed it on top of her bag and then sprinted towards the water's edge to join the others.

Kyla and Ethan were fooling around, splashing and ducking each other, and she waded cautiously into the water, shivering slightly as it surged above her knees. 'I don't know how you two can be so brave. It's freezing.'

'Fresh is the word you're looking for,' Kyla yelled, splashing Ethan and finding herself ducked as a result.

Smiling at the two of them, Evanna gingerly eased herself into the water.

She swam with them for about ten minutes and the cold water was deliciously refreshing against her hot skin. Despite the fact that it was late afternoon, the heat of the sun was relentless.

'All right. That's quite enough exercise. I'm starving.' Kyla rubbed a hand over her face to clear her vision and squinted towards the shore. 'Do you think the food is ready yet?'

'I expect there will be sausages because they always feed the children first.' Evanna dived under the water again, enjoying the cool rush of water through her hair. When she emerged, dripping, Logan was standing in front of her.

Instantly her legs weakened. 'Logan!' Her voice was a shocked squeak. She hadn't expected to see him. Not yet.

More beach bum than doctor, she thought to herself, trying to catch her breath. He was wearing a pair of blue surf shorts and his shoulders were bare.

'Hi, Evanna.' His voice sounded unusually strained and she wiped the water from her eyes and studied him closely.

Something was wrong, she could sense it.

'I— Is everything all right? Where's Kirsty?'

'One of the cousins offered to babysit. I decided to take your advice and have a night out.'

'Oh. Great idea.' He was staring at her. Why was he staring at her? Feeling self-conscious under his steady blue gaze, Evanna lifted a hand and squeezed the water out of her hair. It trailed over her shoulder in a thick, wet rope. 'I tried to call you this morning.'

'You did?' His eyes were on her hair. 'Why?'

She felt hideously flustered, not least because Kyla gave her a wink and started to swim towards shore, leaving her alone with Logan. 'Why did I call you?' She turned away from Kyla, found herself looking at his chest and backed away, flustered. 'Because I wanted to ask about Helen Price. Do you know if she saw the cardiologist?'

'Yes. He confirmed my suspicions. She has an atrial septal defect.'

'Oh, poor thing.' Evanna took another step backwards. 'So what happens now? Open-heart surgery?'

He shook his head. 'They're going to have her in as a day case and operate using a catheter. It should be relatively straightforward.'

'Well, that's progress for you,' Evanna croaked.

He watched her for a long moment and then his eyes slid to her mouth. 'Evanna—' He broke off and lifted his gaze to hers.

For a long moment they stared at each other and she felt her heart hammering rapidly against her chest. There was something in the atmosphere. Something—

No.

She was doing it again! She wasn't going to start imagining something that wasn't there! She wasn't going to start dreaming again!

Anxious to get away from him, she turned towards the shore, her voice bright and breezy as she spoke. 'Well, I've finished my swim so I think I'll go and eat something.'

There was a long, aching silence and then he cleared his throat. 'Go ahead. If you're hungry.'

See? She spoke firmly to herself as she waded to shore. He hadn't even tried to detain her. And what had they spoken about? Work. As usual. It didn't matter whether they were in uniform or swimming gear, their relationship was the same as ever. Professional friendship.

Determined not to wallow, she pulled the blue sundress on top of her damp bikini and left her hair loose. And tonight she wasn't going to spend her evening staring at Logan. She was going to socialise. Mingle. Allow him the space to find the woman he wanted to move on with.

Determined to enjoy herself, she talked to everyone she knew and at least a dozen people who she'd never met before. She spoke at length with Janet Price who was there with Helen, she helped Meg serve the food, she laughed with Kyla as they shared a delicious hamburger, trying not to drip ketchup on their clothes. Then the music started and she kicked off her flip-flops and danced barefoot in the sand with Ethan and then with Nick.

But no matter how much she talked, laughed or danced, she was always aware of Logan standing in the shadows. He danced with no one. Occasionally he exchanged a few words with someone but only when they'd made the effort to approach him. Other than that he stood alone. Apart.

And as midnight approached and lots of families started gathering their things together, Evanna couldn't stand it any longer.

He'd said that he'd forgotten how to approach a woman but surely that couldn't really be the case? Out of the corner of her eye she spotted Polly from the café, laughing at one of Nick's terrible jokes.

Pretty Polly. Wasn't that what all the boys had called her at school? Evanna knew that she'd be only too thrilled to be approached by Logan, so why was he hesitating?

Part of her wanted to leave for her own self-protection but a bigger part of her wanted to see Logan happy.

She walked over to him. 'All you have to do is ask, you know.'

'Ask?'

'You say something like, "Do you fancy joining me for a walk on the beach?"'

'Oh.' He put his drink down on the upturned crate that had been placed on the sand. 'In that case, do you fancy joining me for a walk on the beach?'

Evanna giggled. 'Not me, you idiot. Polly. She's standing there, looking hopeful. If you want to approach her, this is a really good time.'

'But I've already asked you.'

'W-we were j-just practising,' Evanna stammered. 'Role play.'

'All right. In that case, I want you to walk along the beach with me. Call it role play, if you like. It's been so long since I've walked along the beach with a woman, I've forgotten how to do it. I might put my feet in the wrong place.'

There was a dangerous glint in his blue eyes that made her feel strangely uncertain. She couldn't read his thoughts. She really had absolutely no idea what he was thinking. 'Logan, you should be asking Polly.'

'I'm asking you.'

He was obviously still afraid to approach Polly. Deciding that he clearly had no idea just how attractive he was to women, Evanna smiled. 'All right, then. Let's walk. Towards the road or towards the cliffs?'

'The cliffs.' He'd pulled on a loose linen shirt over cut-off shorts but his feet were bare.

'Is it so hard, Logan? Approaching another woman. Is it because you're thinking of Catherine? Does it feel strange? Wrong?' She wanted to understand. *She wanted to help.* Despite the late hour, there was still enough light for her to make out his features.

'I'm not thinking of Catherine. Not at the moment. Should I be?'

'No. I think it's good. But I don't understand why you were reluctant to approach Polly.'

They moved closer to the water's edge and the sea rushed in, swirled around their ankles and then retreated with a gentle hiss.

She glanced back and suddenly realised how far they'd walked. 'I can't see the others.'

'Does that matter?'

'No. I just thought you might want to be getting back so that you can—'

'Are you afraid of the dark?' He gave her a lazy smile and took her hand in his. His fingers closed over hers, his grip strong and firm.

'I'm not afraid of the dark.'

Without announcing his intention, he gave her a gentle pull and started walking away from the sea in the direction of the dunes.

What was he doing? 'Logan—'

'Don't say anything.' His voice sounded strained and suddenly her heart was beating so rapidly that she felt dizzy. This was ridiculous. She was walking hand in hand along a beach with a man she adored. And she didn't have a clue what was going on. *She just didn't know what to say or do.*

They crested the first dune and then slithered and slipped down into the dip. The sea breeze immediately faded away and they were enclosed, cocooned by the gentle swell of sand that created an intimate atmosphere.

'Logan, I really think we should—'

His mouth came down on hers with a hunger that knocked the breath from her body. For a moment Evanna just stood still, so shocked that she couldn't move. She felt the firm pressure of his hand behind her neck, felt his other arm slide round her waist, dragging her hard against him. And then she felt the tip of his tongue demanding an entry and excitement devoured her like a ravenous beast.

Her lips parted against his and she melted into the heat of his kiss, her senses stirred and tumbled as she closed her eyes and sank against him. Shock and surprise melted into frantic excitement. She tried to speak. Tried to reason with him. But his kiss was fierce and greedy and he clearly had no interest in conversation.

With a swift, purposeful movement he undid the tie at the back of her neck and pushed the sundress down over her hips, leaving her in only her skimpy bikini. The air was warm and yet she was shivering uncontrollably and he dragged her closer still, murmuring something incoherent against her mouth.

'Logan...' She didn't know what he was saying. She didn't know what he was thinking. Or what he was doing.

'If you want to stop me, do it now,' he breathed, pulling away from her just long enough to allow him to remove his shirt. He dropped it onto the ground, gently pulled her off balance and lowered her onto the soft mattress of sand. 'Are you going to stop me, Evanna?'

Evanna opened her mouth to suggest that they talk, but he kissed her again and all she was aware of was the hard, male press of his body against hers. Her head was spinning, her thoughts were jumbled and speech suddenly seemed impossible.

'Evanna?' His voice was low and deep and he trailed his mouth over her collarbone, down to her breast.

She felt his fingers pull aside the fabric of her bikini, felt the cool night air touch her exposed nipple and then gasped with shock and agonising pleasure as he took her in his mouth. The skilled flick of his tongue drove hot flashes of fire down her body and she writhed under him in an instinctive attempt to get closer to him. Her hips lifted in an unconsciously feminine gesture of desire and she felt the rigid length of him pressing against her. Hard and ready. He wanted her. Logan wanted her. And she couldn't believe that it was actually happening because although she'd lived this precise moment so often in her dreams, she'd never once allowed herself to believe that it might become reality.

Then he turned his attention to the other breast and all thoughts of reality vanished as the excitement levels became almost unbearable.

She needed him to touch her. Properly. And he obviously knew that because she felt the smooth slide of his hand over her heated flesh and then the subtle movement of his fingers as he removed the final item of her clothing, leaving her naked and exposed.

His fingers cupped her and he paused for a moment, his breathing fractured as he struggled for control. His mouth hovered above hers, their breath mingling as he murmured her name, and then he lowered his head and kissed her again, his fingers moving gently and skilfully until he found that one secret place that was waiting to be discovered.

'Logan, please...' she sobbed against his mouth, and reached down to fumble with his zip, driven by an emotion far more powerful than common sense.

She forgot that they were on a public beach and that others might chose to walk the way that they had walked. For Evanna, the world began and ended with Logan. No one else existed.

'Evanna—my beautiful, gorgeous, Evanna.' His voice was a deep, husky caress and she was so dizzy with excitement that her only response was a shake of her head.

She wasn't his Evanna. Neither was she beautiful or gorgeous, but she didn't even care. All she cared about was now. What he was doing to her. *And what she wanted to do to him.*

Her fingers were on his zip again but he shifted away from her and slid down her trembling, excited body, tasting and touching, using his lips and tongue to expose all her secrets. And he wouldn't let her hide. When she tried to pull him back up her body he gently resisted, pulling away from her seeking fingers, and she felt the rough scrape of male stubble as he moved his lips across her stomach. Then came the gentle nip of his teeth on the inside of her thigh, and finally the skilled flick of his tongue against the nub of her womanhood. And the heat of his mouth and the damp stroke of his tongue felt so maddeningly good that all thoughts of protest evaporated before they'd even formed in her head and she allowed him intimacies that she'd never allowed another man.

And then, when she thought she couldn't stand it any longer, *when she thought she was going to have to beg,* he moved back up her body and slid a strong arm under her hips, raising her slightly. She felt weak and drugged under the skill of his assault and when she felt the blunt tip of his erection brush against her she gave a sob of delicious anticipation. Stopping him was not an option. Instead of stopping, she encouraged him, opening for him, breathing his name against his mouth until he finally thrust into her, entering her by degrees until she was aware of nothing but him, the hardness and the fullness, and she closed her eyes, overwhelmed by the feelings that erupted as he deepened his possession.

For a moment it felt like too much and she ceased to breathe, her body held tense against the fullness and pressure of his.

And then he stilled.

For a moment everything was suspended. Her body was humming with excitement and his elusive male scent made her dizzy with longing.

He lifted his head just enough to speak. 'I just had to be inside you.' As if that were all the explanation that was needed and she didn't even need to question his explanation because she understood.

He gave her time to adjust, allowed her body time to accommodate him, and then he slid a hand through her hair and lowered his mouth to hers in a kiss so possessive that her head spun and excitement spurted. Unable to help herself, Evanna moved her hips and he gave a low grunt of masculine satisfaction and anchored her against him, taking back control.

She slid her hands down his back, over satin-smooth skin and hard male muscle, drawing him still deeper inside her. And still he moved, occasionally withdrawing and then sheathing himself again until his movements became more demanding and he drove them both hard towards completion.

She felt her body explode and tighten around his, heard him mutter something against her mouth and then felt the spasms consume his own body.

And then, finally, peace descended on them.

Lying there in the semi-darkness, Evanna gradually became aware of her surroundings. She heard the soft hiss of the sea and the distant laughter of people enjoying the last moments of the beach barbecue. She smelt sea and sand and healthy, sexy man.

And she couldn't believe what had happened.

She kept her eyes tightly shut, unwilling to open them in case looking somehow broke the spell and returned her to her old life. Because she could never go back, she knew that now.

She'd had so many dreams and none of them had ever come close to the reality of making love with Logan. She'd always thought that she understood what it meant to be close to someone, but suddenly she realised that she hadn't understood at all. She'd been entirely ignorant of the depth of connection that was possible between a man and a woman.

She was aware of him deep inside her, of the fact that he was still hard, and she shifted her hips slightly, enjoying the intimacy.

'Evanna...' His voice hoarse, he lifted his head and brushed his fingers over her cheek. Then he gave a soft curse and moved deeper into her, triggering another set of fireworks in her head. 'I can't let you go. Not yet.'

Why would he want to? She slid her arms round his neck and moved her hips, feeling his instant response.

'We should stop,' she murmured, groaning softly as he moved deeper inside her. 'Someone might walk past.'

'I'm not stopping. No way.'

And she had no real desire to persuade him. 'Then we should move,' she whispered softly, 'somewhere more discreet.'

He didn't reply and she wondered whether he'd even heard her. And then he lifted his mouth from his determined seduction of her breast. 'All right. Your house. It's closer and we don't need the car.'

How they got there she didn't know.

He pushed her bikini in his pocket, pulled her dress over her head, zipped his shorts and slung his shirt over his shoulders. Then he took her hand and propelled her up the path that provided a short cut to her house.

Once inside he barely closed the door before he brought his mouth down on hers again.

Evanna felt her head swim and clutched at his shoulders. 'Logan—the bedroom.'

'Too far.' He scooped her into his arms, carried her into the living room and laid her on the sofa. 'Kiss me.'

And she did.

She wrapped her arms round his neck and felt his hand slide her dress upwards and then he thrust hard inside her and she cried out because it was so perfect.

CHAPTER TEN

WHEN she woke up he was gone.

Evanna sat up slowly, aware that her entire body was aching in a way that it had never ached before. But no one had ever made love to her like that before.

Where had he gone?

When had he gone?

Now that the storm had settled she had so many questions that needed answering, but the biggest was why. Why had he made love to her?

She wanted to believe that what they'd shared was unique and special.

He'd been tender and caring, passionate and demanding all at the same time. Could a man make love like that, *give so much,* and yet feel nothing? Was that possible?

And then she remembered what he'd said that evening she'd talked to him in the garden. He was ready for sex. He'd wanted to have sex with a woman.

And she was that woman.

It hadn't meant anything to him except another step forward in the recovery process. Hadn't he told her that he wasn't interested in a relationship? Hadn't he told her that he wanted sex? Well, finally he'd slept with another woman.

She took a deep breath.

The fact that he'd left before she was awake said everything there was to be said. He was obviously wondering how on earth he was going to deal with the fallout of their night of passion.

Evanna bit her lip and swallowed back the lump in her throat. She needed to let him know that she understood. That she wasn't going to demand anything of him. She'd given him what he'd needed and that was fine.

Except it wasn't fine, was it?

For her, everything had changed.

She'd loved Logan all her life. Lived alongside him. Shared his life. But this was entirely different. What they'd shared couldn't be ignored.

They couldn't just go back to the way they'd been before.

She walked towards the kitchen, stepping over her discarded dress, a cruel reminder of the wild passion of the night before.

In the kitchen, she flicked on the kettle and then stood staring out at the sea.

And suddenly she knew. She knew what had to be done.

She'd deal with Logan and then she'd leave.

She'd leave her beloved Glenmore.

What choice did she have?

Logan was moving on and it was time for her to move on, too. Somewhere else. Somewhere without Logan. She needed to build a new life. While she'd been working on the labour ward in the hospital, they'd made it clear that they'd give her a job any time. She'd call them. Accept the offer.

She glanced around her, realising that moving away would mean selling her precious cottage by the sea.

Change, she reminded herself. Things changed, whether you wanted them to or not. And you had to ride the wave or drown.

* * *

I love you, Evanna.

Slumped in the hammock in the garden, Logan rehearsed the words in his head.

He was stunned by the strength of his feelings. Nothing in his past had prepared him for what he'd felt when he'd made love with Evanna.

So much for all his resolutions about staying away from her. He'd taken one look at her in her bikini and had had red-hot thoughts. So red-hot that he hadn't even been able to look at anyone else all evening, let alone dance with them. Women had approached him, dropping hints, but he'd brushed them all aside as politely as possible. For him, Evanna had been the only woman there. No one else had existed.

Even now his body tightened at the memory of how she'd looked. Her hair had been damp from the water and had hung, glossy and dark, over her bare shoulders. Her eyes had been as dark as sloes, her lashes thick and unbelievably long. And then there had been her mouth.

Logan groaned and closed his eyes.

Her mouth.

Her mouth, curved and laughing at something he'd said. Her mouth parting in shock under his. Her mouth responding, greedily to his demands. *Her mouth touching him...*

He'd been celibate for over a year but he knew that what he'd shared with Evanna had been so much more than just a physical release.

So much more than sex.

They hadn't just shared their bodies. They'd shared *everything.*

And that sharing, *that giving of everything,* had somehow cleared his thoughts and he'd realised at the moment of deepest intimacy just how much he loved Evanna. Just how much he needed her. How much he'd always needed her. Her warmth, her kindness, her endless compassion.

Her gentle hands, her soft mouth and her warm, amazing body.

He'd always thought that what they'd shared had all been about friendship, but he realised now that it was so much more than that.

So much more than he'd imagined possible.

A smile touched his lips. He wished now that he'd called the babysitter and asked her to stay the night. Then he would have been there when Evanna had woken up. He wouldn't have had to wait to tell her that he loved her and he wouldn't have had to wait to look into her eyes and seen that love returned. And he had no doubt that it was returned. Why else would she have responded to him with such unrestrained passion?

Evanna was an old-fashioned girl. She didn't do one-night stands or casual flings. She never had. There was no way she would have allowed him to make love to her unless she had strong feelings. True feelings.

All he had to do now was give her the chance to tell him how she felt.

'Logan?'

Her soft, breathy voice came from right beside him and he felt his body's immediate response.

'Evanna?' He swung his legs out of the hammock and stood up, seeing immediately how nervous she was.

Her hands were clasped in front of her, she was wearing a simple white shirt with a linen skirt and her dark hair was pulled back in a ponytail. Her eyes were shy and there was more than the usual amount of colour in her cheeks.

Her smile faltered, as if she wasn't entirely confident of her reception. 'You were gone when I woke up and I thought we ought to talk.'

She really was nervous and he frowned. 'Evanna—'

'No, wait.' She lifted a hand to cut him off, her smile slightly shaky. 'There are things I have to say and I won't be able to say them if you interrupt. I know you must be worrying about what to say but you really don't need to. Last night was very special to me.' She stumbled over the words and he found himself wondering yet again how he could have taken so long to discover just how much he loved Evanna. She was gorgeous. Incredible.

'It was special to me, too.' He held out a hand but she took a step backwards and gave a little shake of her head, as if to warn him off.

'Don't touch me. Not for a minute. I have to say this and I won't be able to if you touch me.'

With a dark sense of foreboding Logan let his hand drop to his side. 'Have to say what? What is it you have to say, Evanna?' Why wouldn't she let him touch her when they'd spent almost all of last night touching? *Intimately.*

'Last night was a really big step for you. Something you needed to do. And I'm pleased that you chose me.' She stumbled slightly over the words. 'Really pleased that you turned to me. After everything that's happened—it was a really big thing for you. Important. I understand that. A big step in the recovery process. And that's fine.'

He frowned. Recovery process? What was she talking about? She was making an incredible, mind-blowing night of passion sound like some sort of therapy. 'Evanna—'

'We've been friends a long time, Logan. A very long time.'

And he didn't want to be friends any longer. *He wanted so much more than that.* And he'd assumed that she did, too. 'I'm glad you came because I wanted to talk to you. There are things I need to say, too.'

'You don't need to say them, Logan,' she said quickly, her eyes sliding from his. 'We both know how things are. One steamy night isn't going to ruin our friendship. Nothing is going to change. Our friendship is precious and nothing is going to damage that. So we're just going to forget it.'

'Forget it?' He stared at her, stunned by just how sick her words made him feel. He wanted things to change. He wanted everything to change. *He wanted them to be together.* And he certainly didn't want to forget it. 'You want to forget it?' Her fingers were clasped in front of her and he saw that her knuckles were white.

'Of course. I think we should both see it as what it was. An interlude. Hopefully now you'll be able to start going out more. And eventually you'll find someone that you can share you life with.'

So she didn't care for him.

All that giving—*all that loving*—it had been about therapy, Logan thought dully, feeling as though someone had hollowed him out with a sharp knife.

She hadn't slept with him because she loved him but because she cared about his rehabilitation. She felt sorry for him and wanted to help him get over Catherine. What they'd shared had been a sacrifice on her part.

Not love.

Somehow he made his lips move. 'So, that's it, then?'

'Of course. We should just forget it ever happened and you should get out there and start seeing other women. No guilt. No regrets. You know it's what Catherine would have wanted. Life is so fragile, Logan, you should snatch happiness whenever it presents itself.'

He had.

Last night.

'Yes.' He watched as his fresh chance at happiness melted away in front of him. 'Evanna—'

'I really have to go.' She backed away and waved a hand. 'I just didn't want you to feel awkward or embarrassed or anything—I wanted you to know that everything's fine. Fine. No problems.'

She was babbling again, the way she always did when she was nervous, and Logan wanted to drag her into his arms and tell her to stop talking and just kiss him the way she'd kissed him the night before.

But before he could move she turned and walked quickly towards the gate, leaving him staring after her.

Now what?

Now what was he supposed to do?

She'd kept saying that everything was fine. Fine. When everything was far from fine.

After two nights without sleep and a ridiculously busy day during which she'd successfully managed to avoid Logan, Evanna was sitting in her kitchen, wondering whether she even had the energy to drag herself to bed, when the back door flew open and Kyla marched in.

'Is it true?'

Tired and jaded by the events of the weekend, Evanna looked at her warily. How much did she know? 'Is what true?'

'That you're selling the cottage.' Kyla slammed the door shut behind her and glared. 'When did you put your house on the market?'

'Oh.' Evanna blinked several times, surprised at how fast the news had travelled. 'How did you find out?'

'Ed Masters is the only estate agent on the island so it wasn't hard,' Kyla said, her tone sarcastic. 'And I happened to be taking bloods from him today.'

'Word travels fast. I only saw him a few hours ago.'

'He was my last patient of the day. So it's true? You spoke to Ed before you told me?' Kyla put her hands on her hips. 'You're selling your cottage and you didn't think it was worth mentioning? Buy a new lipstick or a pair of shoes, fine. That's information that I don't need to know for a couple of days. But *selling your house? What's going on?*'

'Well, of course I was going to tell you, but—'

'When? After you'd moved?'

Evanna lifted a hand to her forehead, which throbbed and pounded with relentless ferocity. 'Kyla, I don't need this. I'm tired and I'm...' *Miserable, lost, confused.* Her hand dropped to her side and she closed her eyes briefly, blocking out the reality. She still couldn't really take in what selling the house really meant. *She was leaving Glenmore.* 'Yes, I'm selling the cottage.' Saying the words aloud had a finality that unlocked the misery inside her.

'Why? What's happened? You *love* Glenmore. You love your cottage.' Kyla waved a hand and her long blonde hair bounced around her shoulders. 'You've done up every inch of this place exactly the way you like it. It's taken every penny of your salary.'

'Yes.' She didn't need to be reminded exactly how much of herself had gone into this house.

'So why are you selling your house. Your *home?*'

'Because I don't need a home,' Evanna croaked. 'At least, I don't need a home on Glenmore. Not any more.'

Kyla stared. Then she took a deep breath. 'Run that past me again.'

'I'm leaving, Kyla. I've spoken to the Royal Infirmary today and they're going to give me a job on the labour ward. I'm moving to the city. I can start as soon as Logan and Ethan agree to let me go.'

'They'll never agree to let you go and neither will I.' Kyla's voice sounded scratchy and she plopped down onto one of the kitchen chairs. 'Why? Why would you leave Glenmore? You love the island. Why would you go?'

'Because I can't breathe the same air as Logan any more,' Evanna whispered, her expression stricken. 'I have to move on and I've realised that I can't do that when I'm rubbing shoulders with him all the time.'

Kyla was silent. 'Has something happened?'

Evanna hesitated. There were some things too personal to share even with her best friend. 'I just made a decision, that's all.' *After they'd made love for almost all of the night.*

'Does he know?' Kyla's voice was gruff. 'Have you told him?'

'Not yet.' But she was sure he'd be relieved. He wouldn't want her hanging around. It would be too awkward. Evanna walked to the kitchen table and picked up the letter that she'd typed earlier. 'I've redone this a thousand times and I still don't know if it's right.'

'What is it?'

'My letter of resignation.'

'Then it isn't going to be right.' Kyla took it from her and read it swiftly. Then her shoulders sagged and her eyes filled. 'Evanna, don't do this. You're my best friend. You've been my best friend since we pulled each other's hair in toddler group.'

'You pulled my hair,' Evanna mumbled, looking away so that she couldn't see the tears. 'I never touched yours.'

Kyla gave a smile that wasn't entirely steady. 'Yes, well, you always did hate confrontation. You're hopeless at rows because you just want everyone to be friends and love each other. Oh, heck, you're making me cry, and you know I never cry.' She scrabbled in her pocket for a tissue and blew her nose. 'I know I drive you mad but I love you. You're my best friend. What would I do without you?'

'You're married now,' Evanna said softly, blinking back her own tears. 'Everything's different.'

'Being married doesn't alter our friendship.'

'Maybe not. But loving Logan alters everything.'

'Have you told him how you feel about him? Surely it's

worth it before you take such a drastic step? If you're leaving anyway, what does it matter?'

'He knows.' She hadn't told him, but she'd shown him. With her body. *She'd given him everything.* And he hadn't wanted it. Not in the way that she wanted him to want it. He hadn't said a word. Just left while she'd still been sleeping.

'You've spelt it out?'

'We've been here before, Kyla,' Evanna said patiently. 'You can't force someone to love you. Anyway, I don't know why you're being so tragic. You can come and visit me.'

'I'm hopeless in cities,' Kyla muttered, blowing her nose again. 'I get lost and I feel crowded and hemmed in. So do you, you know you do. You've never been a city person and you never will be.'

Evanna took a deep breath. 'You won't change my mind, Kyla,' she said quietly. 'I've been over and over it in my head and I know it's the right thing to do.'

Kyla watched her for a long moment, her eyes swimming with tears. 'Ethan might just beat you up. He hates seeing me cry.'

'I hate seeing you cry, too.' Evanna stood up and held out her arms and Kyla walked into them, hugging her tightly.

'I need Cupid to visit the island and stab my brother. Hard.'

'Yes. It's time he fell in love.'

'I want it to be with you.' Kyla squeezed her hard and then released her. 'I really wanted it to be with you.'

Evanna gave a helpless shrug. 'Life doesn't always turn out the way we want it to. You know that as well as I do. We just have to get on with it. Play the hand we've been given.'

Kyla wiped her face with the palm of her hand and managed a smile. 'You're always so sensible, do you know that? What am I going to do without you? Who is going to stop me eating Meg out of ice cream and chocolate flakes?'

'I never manage to stop you, anyway.' Evanna gave a shaky smile. 'I'll call. And e-mail. We'll stay in touch. I promise.'

'But it won't be the same.'

'No.' Evanna felt her heart twist for everything she was losing. 'No, it won't be the same. But life doesn't stay the same, Kyla. No matter how much you want it to, it doesn't stay the same. We all have to keep moving forward.'

She kept telling herself that.

Keep moving forward.

Logan was just finishing surgery the next morning when his sister marched into the room. One look at the flash in her blue eyes warned him that she was about to pick a fight.

He sighed and sat back in his chair. 'If this is one of your explosions, make it quick. I have house calls.'

'I know. Ellen McBride and Gail Forster. I spoke to Janet. They can both wait.' She slammed the door shut and strode across to his desk. 'Are you seriously going to let her go? She's part of this practice—part of this island—and you're going to let her walk away? Are you nuts?'

Logan blinked. There was nothing quite like his sister in a seething temper. 'I have absolutely no idea what you're talking about,' he drawled softly, and she glared at him.

'Well, of course you haven't. You're obviously *completely* stupid.'

He lifted an eyebrow. 'And your evidence for that assessment would be—?'

'The fact that you're letting Evanna leave! How could you do it? How *could* you let her resign? She belongs here. She belongs with us. She's part of Glenmore Island. Part of the practice. You'll never find another nurse like her if you search high and low!'

Logan sat still. 'What do you mean, leave? Where's she going?'

'To the mainland. To work. And live. And...' Kyla faltered

and waved a hand. 'To do all the things that she used to do here. Did you accept her letter of resignation? Did you?'

'She's planning to resign?' Logan rose to his feet and Kyla folded her arms across her chest and narrowed her eyes.

'You're pretending that you don't know?'

'Of course I didn't know,' he snapped, and then drew in a deep breath and forced himself to think. This was all his fault. He'd compromised her. He'd destroyed their friendship. If she was leaving, it was because of him. 'It's my fault, Kyla.'

'Well, I know *that*. The whole thing is your fault.'

Logan frowned. She knew? Evanna had told her? It was true that Kyla and Evanna were close friends, but still... 'I'm not in the habit of discussing my sex life with my sister.'

'Your sex life? Why would I want to discuss your sex life?' Kyla threw him an impatient glance. 'I mean, it isn't as if you—' She broke off and stared at him. 'What did you just say?'

'I said that I'm not prepared to discuss my sex life with you.'

'We were talking about Evanna.'

'Yes.'

Kyla stared and then swallowed. 'You had sex with Evanna? You—'

Logan's gaze was icy. 'I've already told you, I won't discuss my sex life. If Evanna chose to confide in you, that's up to her, but—'

'She didn't.' Kyla sat down in the nearest chair and stared at the wall. 'She didn't, but now I see. You had sex? When?'

'Kyla!'

'Just tell me!' Kyla's voice was a threatening growl. 'For goodness' sake, this is important. When?'

He let out a long breath. 'The night of the barbecue.'

'Saturday.' Kyla gave a slow nod. 'That explains everything.'

'Does it?'

'Of course it does. Sex changes everything. Up until the sex part she was perfectly able to live with the fact that she loved you and you didn't love her back. But sex—sex for Evanna is extremely serious. Evanna doesn't do casual relationships.'

'I know that. I...' He frowned at her, trying to decipher the strange conversation they were having. 'Did you just say that she was able to live with the fact that she loved me, but I didn't love her back?'

'Yes. After both plan A and plan B failed, she decided to just give up and live with things as they are.' Kyla's tone was conversational and then she glanced up and saw the darkening expression on her brother's face. 'What?'

His tone was dangerously soft. 'I'd like to hear the details of plan A and plan B.'

Kyla squirmed. 'I probably shouldn't—'

'I'll give you five seconds to start talking.'

Kyla sighed. 'Oh, well, given that the whole thing is such a mess, I don't see any harm in it.'

She was going to miss Glenmore Island so much.

Evanna sat on the cliffs and stared across the sea towards the mainland. It was a view she'd grown up with. A view she'd believed she'd grow old with.

She couldn't imagine not seeing it on a daily basis as she drove to work. She couldn't imagine not popping into Meg's café for a coffee and a gossip. She couldn't imagine not running along the cliffs, swimming in the sea and sharing barbecues in Logan's garden with all their friends and family.

But she needed to build a new life and that was what she was going to do.

Somehow she'd struggled through her morning clinic, seeing patients on automatic, responding to their questions without even hearing her own answers. She'd intended to go straight into Logan's room and tell him her plans but instead she'd found herself walking up here to the cliffs for one last look.

Her letter of resignation sat in her pocket like a lump of lead.

After Kyla had left the previous evening, she'd read it over and over again and cried so hard that she'd thought her head might burst.

Then she'd made a supreme effort to pull herself together. Enough.

Enough crying.

'Evanna?'

She turned and saw him standing there, his hair lifting in the breeze, his face so handsome that it made her catch her breath. 'Logan? What are you doing up here?'

His gaze was fixed on her face, his blue eyes sharply questioning. 'I should be asking you the same question.'

'Oh.' She scrambled to her feet and struggled to produce a smile. 'I just needed some fresh air.'

'Why would you need fresh air?' His eyes didn't shift from hers and she felt her stomach roll over.

Now. She should tell him now. It was the perfect opportunity. 'I—I'm glad you came up here. I was hoping to catch up with you later. I needed to give you something.' Her hand shaking, she delved into her pocket and pulled out the crumpled letter. 'Sorry. It's been in my pocket.' She thrust it towards him and he took it and tore it in half in a slow, purposeful movement and then handed it back to her.

She stared at him in confusion and then looked at the torn letter in her hand. 'You didn't even read it.'

'I didn't need to.' His voice was steady. 'I know what was in that letter, Evanna, and the answer is no. You're not resigning. You're not leaving Glenmore Island, you're not leaving the practice and most of all you're not leaving me.'

She stared at him and felt the emotion surge up inside her

again. He was being so unfair. This was hard enough for her without him making it even harder. 'I suppose Kyla told you. You can't stop me, Logan.' She almost choked on the words. 'I know it's inconvenient for you, but I'm not the only nurse in the world. You'll find someone else who can do the job just as well.'

'That isn't true. I wouldn't find a nurse as good as you if I searched Scotland, but that isn't why I'm not going to let you go.'

She gave a helpless shrug. 'Are you thinking of Kirsty? Because you needn't worry about that. I'll stay in touch.'

'It isn't about Kirsty.'

'I can't stay, Logan.' Her voice was a whisper. 'I have to go. I— It's complicated.'

'I've never minded complicated. Why do you have to go, Evanna?'

Their eyes held for a long moment and then she turned away and looked at the sea. 'That doesn't really matter.'

'It matters to me.'

'Why?' She swallowed hard and concentrated on the antics of a seagull swooping down to snatch a tidbit from the water.

'Because we have a relationship.' He gave soft curse and she felt his hands on her arms, his grip firm and purposeful as he turned her towards him. 'For goodness' sake, look at me, Evanna! This conversation is hard enough without trying to talk to your back. I want to know why you feel you have to leave the island. You owe me an explanation. And I want the truth.'

Given no alternative, she lifted her eyes to his face. He looked rough and rugged, strands of dark hair flopping over his forehead, his blue eyes sharp and observant. She'd grown up looking at his face. *Seen him grow from boy to man.* 'There's nothing more I can tell you, Logan.'

'No?' His eyes were very blue. 'You're not going to tell me exactly how long you've been in love with me? How long, Evanna?'

Her heart tripped over and she stood still, aware of his gaze on her face. Above them a seagull shrieked, but neither of them noticed. 'For ever.' The word was barely audible so she cleared her throat and tried again. 'For ever, Logan. I've been in love with you for ever. Girl, teenager and woman. There. You wanted the truth and now you have it.' She waited to feel humiliation or embarrassment but instead all she felt was relief. Finally there was no longer any need to pretend.

His gaze didn't flicker. 'And you're leaving because...?'

'I've just told you why I'm leaving.'

'No, you haven't. You told me that you love me. Girl, teenager and woman. You haven't told me why you're leaving.'

'How can you be so insensitive? I can't be this close to you any more. It hurts too much. I want to find a family, a home, a man who loves me, and I'm never going to find those things while you're in my line of vision because no one else exists for me.'

There was a long silence broken only by the distant rush of waves over rock. Then he let go of her arms and took her face in his hands. 'Look at me. I want you to look at me.'

'No.' She closed her eyes. 'This is so hard for me, Logan.'

'Then let me make it easier. I want you looking at me when I tell you that I love you, too. I love you, Evanna.' He stroked her face with his fingers and she opened her eyes.

'What did you say?'

'I love you. I should have told you the night we made love but you fell asleep and I had to get back to Kirsty. And then the next morning I was ready to tell you and you started talking about how much you wanted us to still be friends.'

She looked into his eyes, those lazy blue eyes that always made her weak at the knees. 'We had sex, Logan. It wasn't about love.'

'Yes, it was. It was all about love.' He gave a crooked smile and she felt suddenly peculiar. Her heart was hammering and her pulse was dancing. But she pushed down the little spurt of excitement.

'You've known me all your life, Logan. I'm sure you do love me. Like a sister.'

'*Not* like a sister.' His gaze dropped to her mouth and lingered there. 'Nothing like a sister.'

It was becoming hard to breathe. 'I've been under your nose for ever.'

'So maybe I'm just a bit slow.' He stroked her hair away from her face with a gentle hand. 'Or maybe, subconsciously, I always thought that you were out of bounds. You were my baby sister's best friend. Then you were a colleague.'

'You've kissed just about every girl on this island, Logan MacNeil. But you never kissed me until last Saturday.'

'If I'd known how good it was going to be, I would have been kissing you in the playground, right under Ann Carne's nose.' He hesitated. 'Perhaps I didn't kiss you because you were the only one that mattered to me. Our relationship was too important to risk messing it all up.'

She couldn't listen. *She couldn't allow herself to believe it.* 'Logan, you've had a terrible year, and—'

'Stop.' He covered her lips with his fingers. 'If you're going to suggest that this is rebound or therapy or anything like that, don't waste your breath. What I feel for you is real, Evanna. And it's for ever.'

'But—'

'It doesn't make sense, does it? You're going to ask me why I suddenly know I love you when you've always been in my life. Why haven't I felt it before? And I don't know the answer to that. I don't know why I haven't realised it before.'

'You loved Catherine.'

'Yes, I did.' His voice was soft. 'I won't lie to you about that. I did love Catherine. But she's gone. And now I'm in love with you. I'm crazy about you and I can't let you leave the island. You told me that I should grab happiness and I agree with you. But you're my happiness, Evanna.'

She struggled to speak. 'Logan…' Her voice shook and she tried again. 'I've dreamed about you for so long—wanted you for so long…'

'I never knew. I never knew that you felt like that.' He gave a groan and lowered his mouth to hers, his kiss warm and insistent. Then he lifted his head just enough to speak. 'I must be blind and stupid. Will you marry me?'

How could it happen? How could a person go from misery to happiness in one bound? 'It's too soon—you need time to think about things.'

He shook his head. 'Evanna, I've known you for twenty-six years. How much more time do you think I need? Will you be my wife? Will you be a mother to my daughter?'

Kirsty.

Tears filled her eyes. 'I've wanted this for so long I can't believe that it's true.'

'Believe it.' He muttered the words against her mouth. 'And then say yes. You said that you wanted a home and a family, a man who loves you, here on Glenmore Island. You have it, Evanna. If you want it, it's all yours.'

She slid her arms round his neck and buried her face in his neck. 'I want it. I want everything.' She lifted her head and melted into the heat of his kiss, excitement burning away the exhaustion and misery of the past few days. 'I love you, Logan. I can't believe you want me to be your wife and a mother to Kirsty. And your practice nurse.'

He gave a slow smile. 'For now.'

'What do you mean, for now?'

He kissed her once again. 'You can be my practice nurse until I find you something better to do. I'm planning on keeping you fairly busy in the bedroom, Evanna MacNeil. We're going to have a large family.'

'Really?'

'Really.' He brushed his lips over hers. 'How many children is a good number, do you think? Nine? Ten?'

She giggled. 'Ann Carne would have a fit if we gave her ten little MacNeil children to teach.'

His eyes gleamed. 'We have a duty to maintain the population of rural communities.'

Evanna felt a warm glow of happiness. It felt as though someone had touched her dreams with a magic wand and turned them into reality. 'You called me Evanna MacNeil. Have you any idea how many times I scribbled that name in my textbooks?'

'Did you? Well, I'm glad to hear it.' His mouth was still close to hers. 'It means that you won't need any practice writing it down once we're married.'

Her heart jumped. 'Married...'

'Yes, married. I love you, Evanna Duncan MacNeil. Are you going to say yes to me?'

'Yes.' She smiled and smiled. 'Yes. Yes. Yes-s-s.'

0307 Gen Std HB

MILLS & BOON®

Live the emotion

APRIL 2007 HARDBACK TITLES

ROMANCE™

The Ruthless Marriage Proposal *Miranda Lee* 978 0 263 19604 7
Bought for the Greek's Bed *Julia James* 978 0 263 19605 4
The Greek Tycoon's Virgin Mistress *Chantelle Shaw*
978 0 263 19606 1
The Sicilian's Red-Hot Revenge *Kate Walker* 978 0 263 19607 8
The Italian Prince's Pregnant Bride *Sandra Marton*
978 0 263 19608 5
Kept by the Spanish Billionaire *Cathy Williams* 978 0 263 19609 2
The Kristallis Baby *Natalie Rivers* 978 0 263 19610 8
Mediterranean Boss, Convenient Mistress *Kathryn Ross*
978 0 263 19611 5
A Mother for the Tycoon's Child *Patricia Thayer*
978 0 263 19612 2
The Boss and His Secretary *Jessica Steele* 978 0 263 19613 9
Billionaire on her Doorstep *Ally Blake* 978 0 263 19614 6
Married by Morning *Shirley Jump* 978 0 263 19615 3
Princess Australia *Nicola Marsh* 978 0 263 19616 0
The Sheikh's Contract Bride *Teresa Southwick* 978 0 263 19617 7
The Surgeon and the Single Mum *Lucy Clark* 978 0 263 19618 4
The Surgeon's Longed-For Bride *Emily Forbes* 978 0 263 19619 1

HISTORICAL ROMANCE™

A Scoundrel of Consequence *Helen Dickson* 978 0 263 19757 0
An Innocent Courtesan *Elizabeth Beacon* 978 0 263 19758 7
The King's Champion *Catherine March* 978 0 263 19759 4

MEDICAL ROMANCE™

Single Father, Wife Needed *Sarah Morgan* 978 0 263 19796 9
The Italian Doctor's Perfect Family *Alison Roberts*
978 0 263 19797 6
A Baby of Their Own *Gill Sanderson* 978 0 263 19798 3
His Very Special Nurse *Margaret McDonagh*
978 0 263 19799 0

MILLS & BOON®

Live the emotion

0307 Gen Std LP

APRIL 2007 LARGE PRINT TITLES

ROMANCE™

The Christmas Bride *Penny Jordan*	978 0 263 19439 6
Reluctant Mistress, Blackmailed Wife *Lynne Graham*	
	978 0 263 19440 X
At the Greek Tycoon's Pleasure *Cathy Williams*	978 0 263 19441 8
The Virgin's Price *Melanie Milburne*	978 0 263 19442 6
The Bride of Montefalco *Rebecca Winters*	978 0 263 19443 4
Crazy about the Boss *Teresa Southwick*	978 0 263 19444 2
Claiming the Cattleman's Heart *Barbara Hannay*	
	978 0 263 19445 0
Blind-Date Marriage *Fiona Harper*	978 0 263 19446 9

HISTORICAL ROMANCE™

An Improper Companion *Anne Herries*	978 0 263 19388 8
The Viscount *Lyn Stone*	978 0 263 19389 6
The Vagabond Duchess *Claire Thornton*	978 0 263 19390 X

MEDICAL ROMANCE™

Rescue at Cradle Lake *Marion Lennox*	978 0 263 19343 8
A Night to Remember *Jennifer Taylor*	978 0 263 19344 6
The Doctors' New-Found Family *Laura MacDonald*	
	978 0 263 19345 4
Her Very Special Consultant *Joanna Neil*	978 0 263 19346 2
A Surgeon, A Midwife: A Family *Gill Sanderson*	978 0 263 19537 6
The Italian Doctor's Bride *Margaret McDonagh*	978 0 263 19538 4

0407 Gen Std HB

MILLS & BOON®

MAY 2007 HARDBACK TITLES

ROMANCE™

Bought: The Greek's Bride *Lucy Monroe*   978 0 263 19620 7
The Spaniard's Blackmailed Bride *Trish Morey*
   978 0 263 19621 4
Claiming His Pregnant Wife *Kim Lawrence*   978 0 263 19622 1
Contracted: A Wife for the Bedroom *Carol Marinelli*
   978 0 263 19623 8
Willingly Bedded, Forcibly Wedded *Melanie Milburne*
   978 0 263 19624 5
Count Giovanni's Virgin *Christina Hollis*   978 0 263 19625 2
The Millionaire Boss's Baby *Maggie Cox*   978 0 263 19626 9
The Italian's Defiant Mistress *India Grey*   978 0 263 19627 6
The Forbidden Brother *Barbara McMahon*   978 0 263 19628 3
The Lazaridis Marriage *Rebecca Winters*   978 0 263 19629 0
Bride of the Emerald Isle *Trish Wylie*   978 0 263 19630 6
Her Outback Knight *Melissa James*   978 0 263 19631 3
The Cowboy's Secret Son *Judy Christenberry*   978 0 263 19632 0
Best Friend...Future Wife *Claire Baxter*   978 0 263 19633 7
A Father for Her Son *Rebecca Lang*   978 0 263 19634 4
The Surgeon's Marriage Proposal *Molly Evans*   978 0 263 19635 1

HISTORICAL ROMANCE™

Dishonour and Desire *Juliet Landon*   978 0 263 19760 0
An Unladylike Offer *Christine Merrill*   978 0 263 19761 7
The Roman's Virgin Mistress *Michelle Styles*   978 0 263 19762 4

MEDICAL ROMANCE™

Single Dad, Outback Wife *Amy Andrews*   978 0 263 19800 3
A Wedding in the Village *Abigail Gordon*   978 0 263 19801 0
In His Angel's Arms *Lynne Marshall*   978 0 263 19802 7
The French Doctor's Midwife Bride *Fiona Lowe*
   978 0 263 19803 4

MILLS & BOON®

0407 Gen Std LP

MAY 2007 LARGE PRINT TITLES

ROMANCE™

The Italian's Future Bride *Michelle Reid*	978 0 263 19447 0
Pleasured in the Billionaire's Bed *Miranda Lee*	978 0 263 19448 7
Blackmailed by Diamonds, Bound by Marriage *Sarah Morgan*	978 0 263 19449 4
The Greek Boss's Bride *Chantelle Shaw*	978 0 263 19450 0
Outback Man Seeks Wife *Margaret Way*	978 0 263 19451 7
The Nanny and the Sheikh *Barbara McMahon*	978 0 263 19452 4
The Businessman's Bride *Jackie Braun*	978 0 263 19453 1
Meant-To-Be Mother *Ally Blake*	978 0 263 19454 8

HISTORICAL ROMANCE™

Not Quite a Lady *Louise Allen*	978 0 263 19391 6
The Defiant Debutante *Helen Dickson*	978 0 263 19392 3
A Noble Captive *Michelle Styles*	978 0 263 19393 0

MEDICAL ROMANCE™

The Christmas Marriage Rescue *Sarah Morgan*	978 0 263 19347 3
Their Christmas Dream Come True *Kate Hardy*	978 0 263 19348 0
A Mother in the Making *Emily Forbes*	978 0 263 19349 7
The Doctor's Christmas Proposal *Laura Iding*	978 0 263 19350 3
Her Miracle Baby *Fiona Lowe*	978 0 263 19539 2
The Doctor's Longed-for Bride *Judy Campbell*	978 0 263 19540 8